Audra

AMANDA L.V. SHALABY

author of *Rhianna*

CRIMSON
ROMANCE
F+W Media, Inc.

This edition published by
Crimson Romance
an imprint of F+W Media, Inc.
10151 Carver Road, Suite 200
Blue Ash, Ohio 45242
www.crimsonromance.com

ISBN 10: 1-4405-6709-3
ISBN 13: 978-1-4405-6709-4
eISBN 10: 1-4405-6710-7
eISBN 13: 978-1-4405-6710-0

*For Matt, who now knows more about nineteenth-century
England than he ever expected he would.
For Dad, for attempting it.
For Mom, always.
And for Bella, who healed a broken heart.*

Acknowledgments

A massive thank you to Jennifer Lawler and everyone at Crimson Romance who worked so hard to make both *Rhianna* and *Audra* a reality. I wouldn't have wanted to do it without you.

A very special thank you to Jennifer for taking a chance on me and always making me feel you love my stories as much as I do.

Chapter One

February, 1836—Thornton, England

"Lady Audra, wake up. It's time."

The voice was a distant echo. Its urgency held no power over the softness of her pillow, and Audra turned her back to the direction it had come.

Suddenly, a firm hand came to rest on her shoulder. "Lady Audra, if you want to come, you must get dressed with haste."

Audra's eyelashes fluttered, and her head turned over her shoulder to the flickering halo of candlelight around her beloved governess. "Miss Mauvreen?"

The shadows cast over Mauvreen's face made her wrinkles appear far deeper than they, in fact, were. The room outside the reach of the halo was dark, and a stillness betrayed the midnight hour.

"The carriage leaves imminently. It is happening."

Audra stretched her legs and let out a soft sigh. "What is happening?"

Mauvreen cupped Audra's cheek in her hand. "Lady Rhianna Brighton is in labor."

• • •

Audra insisted she be present for the birth of the child, against Miss Mauvreen's advice. She was glad to find, despite their reservations, that both Miss Mauvreen and Rhianna were honoring her request. Even if the experience threatened to leave her forever scarred and wishing no part in having any children of her own, Audra was willing even to take that chance to be at her half sister's side.

Of course, in the world's view, she and Rhianna were not sisters. Until her sixteenth birthday, Audra herself had not known that the fair-skinned, redheaded governess who had come into her life at the age of twelve had the same blood running through her veins as she did. No, until a future date when Audra married Rhianna's younger brother-in-law, Lord Crispin Brighton, they would not be sisters, save in the eyes of a few who knew the truth.

Oh, that she were married to Crispin already! Audra reminded herself that she must first come out in Society before she could marry anyone at all—an event imminent enough. As the upcoming Season approached, Audra knew her time to be introduced to Society was only months away. Perhaps this time next year, she would be having a baby of her own…

She pushed these thoughts aside, as the more immediate birth of her niece or nephew lay ahead of her. Audra looked enthusiastically out the window of the bouncing carriage for a glimpse of Ravensleigh, her sister's home with her husband, Lord Thayne Brighton, his mother, Lady Moira Brighton, and of course, Lord Crispin. The battlements of Ravensleigh silhouetted in the moonlight of the small hours announced the nearness of the country manor house.

Audra was anxious to arrive. For four years, her sister had been unable to conceive. Once she did become pregnant, the pregnancy was a difficult one. Audra visited Rhianna frequently, as she had been confined to her bed these last months. No one who knew the story of her mother's maternal death spoke of the fear Rhianna would suffer a similar fate, but the fear afflicted all. The previous weeks had been especially stressful as the time for the birth drew nearer. At home, Audra often found their father, Guilford, Lord Kingsley, staring blankly at the wall of his study from his mahogany leather chair. Miss Mauvreen, who had herself been midwife to Rhianna's mother, often failed at attempts to be strong before her. At Ravensleigh, Rhianna's husband, Thayne, was entirely unable to hold conversation. His mother, Lady Moira Brighton, a woman who expressed a love for her daughter-in-law as if she were of her own womb grew paler by the day. And Audra was not unaffected. With the loss of her own mother and elder brother just four years ago, her heart was ill prepared to lose the sister she had only recently gained. Happily, for all her discomfort, Rhianna had been in remarkably good spirits all along, and everyone drew a small comfort from knowing there was never a mother-to-be who so enjoyed her pregnancy regardless of its challenges.

Audra wondered how she would find her sister on this night, however, and was quick to stand as the carriage came to a wavering halt. Her silent companion rose with her. After all, it was Mauvreen that Rhianna had requested to be at her side. Though Mauvreen was too old to assist with the delivery, Audra understood the significant history between them, and that Mauvreen's presence as a long-time friend and confidant to Rhianna, not to mention the woman who had attended Rhianna's own birth, would bring her sister comfort.

The lanterns were still swinging about the vehicle when Audra and Mauvreen alighted. With careful footing on the dimly lit ground, they ascended Ravensleigh's wide front steps and met the butler, Remford, at the door. There, Audra did not wait to be led to Rhianna's room, but left Mauvreen in Remford's care to follow at her own, slower pace, and raced up the stairs to her sister's bedside.

• • •

Assisting the fireplace, a profusion of candles lay scattered about the dressing table, a chest of drawers, a wardrobe, and every small table, lighting the room as if it were day. Rhianna lay in the center of a wooden, four-post bed, her husband Thayne kneeling at her side. The long, red curls that lay strewn across her pillows were a stark contrast to Rhianna's fair skin that paled further against the white sheets around her, the Irish blood stronger in Rhianna than in Audra.

"Dear sister!" Audra took her place opposite Thayne and kissed Rhianna's cheek. Laying an affectionate hand on her shoulder, she said, "Miss Mauvreen is on her way up. How are you doing?"

"I will be most glad for this to be over with," Rhianna told her in a weary voice. "The doctor says it will be some time yet."

Audra could not tell which one of the expectant parents was perspiring more. "Lord Brighton," she addressed, "how are *you* doing?"

Thayne was undoing several buttons on his white shirt, as if it battled to choke him to death. "I also will be most glad for this to be over with."

"You really don't need to stay for this," Rhianna told her, her tone dripping with the sweetness of one who knew the dark thoughts haunting her relatives and was determined to quell them with positive reassurance. "I am sure I will be quite fine. We are created for this, you know."

As she spoke, Audra watched Rhianna's hand compress over her bulging stomach, and she tightened her own stomach muscles in response. Turning her eyes back to Rhianna's face, Audra unwittingly imitated her sister's strained expression, tightening her jaw and tucking her chin to her chest.

"I refuse to leave under any circumstances," Audra said definitively. She forced her chin upward, determined to both look and sound brave—a tower of strength for her dear one. "Now, what am I to call this child of yours? Have you decided?"

Rhianna's eyes lit up and met Thayne's gaze briefly. "James Edward, if it is a boy," she said, smiling. "If it is a girl, Isabella Catherine."

Audra's heart fluttered as the names brought the child ever closer to reality. Fleetingly, she wondered if the baby would look something like what a child of hers and Crispin's would look like.

Rhianna lurched forward with a powerful contraction, and Audra's heart somersaulted right into her throat. The growling cry that escaped through Rhianna's clenched teeth was a foreign sound that brought with it a lightning bolt to Audra's spine. She stiffened, not knowing what to do, and was glad when Miss Mauvreen entered the room, followed by Dr. Logan.

Audra quickly went from feeling brave to helpless. Too, she felt horrified, as the doctor was at once between Rhianna's exposed legs, feeling her progress with his fingers. She met the doctor's eyes briefly, and he seemed surprised to see her there. She was grateful to switch places with Mauvreen, who pressed a damp cloth to Rhianna's face and neck. Perhaps her governess was right—she ought not to see this. But Audra would not leave now. From her new vantage point, she watched Rhianna's toes curl into the bed sheets, and Audra took a deep breath, readying herself for a night she would surely never forget.

• • •

Audra stood by the window, the late morning sunlight pouring over her as she softly rocked the newborn baby boy to and fro as he slept in her arms. Beside her, Rhianna, too, slept soundly in her bed, the doctor long since gone. Thayne dozed on and off in a corner chair. It was a peaceful moment. In only a few hours, the months of stress gave way to relief as the fears associated with the pregnancy were dissolved. The delivery had been a success, and the hours since the blessing of James' birth had been filled with nothing but unmitigated joy.

James Edward Brighton, the heir to Ravensleigh, was wrapped snugly in a knitted, ivory blanket, with nothing but his peaches-and-cream face exposed to his Aunt Audra's proud eyes. She wondered how long it would be before Lady Brighton returned to claim her grandson. Until then, Audra was resolved to enjoy him, and she marveled as his tiny nostrils expanded gently with each soft breath. A tuft of black hair already covered the crown of his little, round head while a matching set of familiar black eyelashes contrasted handsomely against his fair skin.

Yes, thought Audra, *he is most certainly a Brighton.*

Suddenly, a strong, motherly yearning stole over her. Yes, a burning desire to produce an heir to her own Kingsley Manor seemed more vitally necessary than ever before. Thank heavens there was another Brighton ready to fulfill his role in the equation.

Now, she just needed to marry him.

Chapter Two

"But, Papa, it really seems quite silly, since I am going to marry Crispin."

Audra paced from one end of her father's burgundy-themed study to the other, until the warmth from the marble-framed fireplace finally enticed her to be still. On turning to face him, she dropped her arms to her sides, wondering how she had ever allowed her hands to make their way to her hips, and did her best to appear docile.

Guilford, Lord Kingsley extended his hand across his chestnut desk to the leather, scroll-backed chair opposite. "Audra, dear, have a seat."

He held out his hand until she relented to his invitation. She wanted to stomp her way across the room, but reminded herself she was nearly seventeen now. Propriety must restrain her. Thus, she made her way gracefully to the chair—but propriety could only take her so far. Audra plopped into the seat with all her weight, her skirts fluttering about her with sudden commotion.

"Why can I not come out at home?" Audra asked. "We can have my coming out ball right here at Kingsley Manor. It would be the simplest thing in the world."

Guilford leaned back in his chair and she could see he was prepared to wait patiently for her speech, however long—but to what end? Knowing her father would eventually have his say; Audra forced a submissive comportment and allowed him the floor without further petition. Despite a keen desire for things to go her way, she respected her father's opinion above all others, and told herself not only to hear him, but to listen.

"My dear Audra," he began, folding his hands peacefully over a generous midriff that had replaced the sickly frame that had been his four years ago, "while I do feel you have seen little of the world, and I hate to watch you give up having any Season at all, I do know you love Lord Crispin. The Brightons are an established, respectable family, and I have no objection to you marrying him, as I had no objection to your sister marrying into the name before you."

This statement dramatically lifted her spirits, and his relaxed, conciliatory demeanor put her at ease. Feeling sure of her victory in the argument, Audra began to settle into her seat.

"So why would you insist that I go to London?" she asked, as if they both now saw the suggestion as a mere distant thought.

He eyed her with a familiar, amused gaze. "I may be up in years, but I can still remember a sprightly, five-year-old girl who dreamed passionately of being presented at St. James and practiced her full-court curtsey in this very room." He smiled at the recollection. "You may not think it necessary at the moment, but I do not mean to see you regret it later on. Do you want to be the only girl of your station *not* to be presented at St. James?"

Audra looked away and considered this, her conviction of triumph waning sharply. Indeed, she mourned her imagined rise to victory, and marveled at how a single sentence had plummeted her hopes to the depths of defeat.

Her father continued, "I see no reason why you cannot go to London, have your presentation at court, a ball at Almack's, and then return to Thornton. Do you doubt that Lord Crispin would wait for you?"

"No, Papa," she said. "It's just…Oh, for heaven's sake, it's just so *inconvenient!*"

Again, her feet demanded permission to stomp on the wood floor of the study, but she fought them vehemently. If ever there was a time to behave as a lady, this was it, and she commanded her inner childlike urges to their corner.

"Things that are worth doing are rarely convenient, my dear. Even still, Lord Thayne Brighton has generously offered his London townhouse to you, and Lady Moira Brighton has found you a sponsor. The circumstances are not as inconvenient as you make it sound."

She crossed her arms over her lap in as womanly a fashion as she could muster and straightened her spine so that she might sit as tall in her chair as her small stature would allow.

"You know, I may never have desired to go if it hadn't been for Mama filling my head with the idea. I cannot say for sure if I ever really wanted to go of my own initiative."

This was unfair, and she felt regret at saying it. Even as she spoke the words, she felt the bitterness of them on her palate and wished she could have caught them before they escaped her lips. Any mention of her deceased mother was unpleasant to her father, and both of them knew her desire to be a debutante at St. James was her own. But four years after she had fallen in love with him, Audra was well ready to marry Lord Crispin, and she had not one whit of patience for delay.

In the end, it was contrition for turning a sharp tongue to her beloved father that forced a relenting spirit from her.

"I did not mean that," she told him, rolling back against her chair and preparing her heart for acquiescence. "You are right. I have been dreaming about St. James since I was a little girl. I should go to London and see it through."

She said it with finality. Audra was not one to drag out decisions, and her father nodded cheerily at the verdict.

"Do me a favor, would you, Audra?" She cast him a sidelong glance, resigned to her fate so swiftly, so absolutely, it was quite as if she had intended all along to go. "Allow yourself to enjoy it."

•••

"Lord, Audra, I don't see at all why you should go to London," said Crispin, as they braved the chilly weather to walk along one of Ravensleigh's garden paths.

The liberties they took with each other's Christian names were nothing short of natural to them. Audra had briefly attempted to call him "Lord Crispin" when she was twelve years of age, but it simply would not stick. His own efforts to call her "Lady Audra" were an equal failure, attempted on the very same day when he was sixteen years of age, and not a single day since.

As she strolled beside Crispin, Audra undid the ribbons of her blue bonnet and removed it with decided dislike. Her corset was restrictive enough; the bonnet had to go. Surely they were far enough into the gardens that Miss Mauvreen would not see to tell her otherwise.

"That is because *you* are not a young woman about to come out in society," she returned, smiling.

The moment it was settled that she should go, Audra had taken to heart her father's advice to enjoy the experience. It was her nature to embrace her decisions passionately, and she could no longer find any fault with the plan.

"You had your levee. You should understand," she added.

Crispin's hands were pressed deep into his pockets as he moped along the path. "Well, you don't have to look so happy about it."

Audra's bell-like laugh floated through the air. "Why shouldn't I be happy about it?"

There was no hint of a smile on Crispin's face. Audra turned to him, stared into the sky-blue eyes that were a bottomless pit of concern, and lifted a playful eyebrow.

"Because the moment you are presented at St. James," he told her, "every bloke in the city is going to be throwing themselves at you. They're going to think you're theirs for the taking."

"Is that so?"

"It is."

Audra, considering his unconcealed jealousy with no small amount of pleasure, walked on, spinning her bonnet by the ribbons.

Wishing to offer him some relief, she said, "You realize, of course, I could be *no one's* for the taking without coming out first."

Crispin shot her a side glance that told her he understood her meaning.

"I shall see you before you know it," she added cheerfully, as if the whole matter had never been a concern to her at all. In fact, she *had* forgotten it was of any previous concern to her, and indeed quite liked the idea of going to London.

"Certainly," he said, turning his gaze to the horizon and stepping toward it as if he were walking the plank. "After you've attended fifty balls, parties, and dinners and quickened the pulse of more gentlemen than I care to envision."

At this, Audra caught him by the arm, and they halted. "Crispin." She took his face in her hands, and, forcing him to meet her eyes, professed, "They shall not quicken mine."

For a time, they gazed at one another in silence, and Audra allowed the power of her words to make their imprint on his heart.

Only once she was convinced he had felt the full effect of them did she add, "Besides, I see no reason to stay in London once I am presented. I have every intention of coming home as soon as the whole business is done."

"How do you know you will not fall in love with London and want to stay longer?"

"Because *you* are not in London."

Audra hoisted herself onto her toes and stole a quick kiss from him. It happened so quickly that, by the time Crispin had closed his eyes, it was over. Audra was pleased to find he did not rush them open.

When at last he did look at her again, he asked, "Do you remember our first kiss, Audra?"

She rested her thumbs where a smile played about the corners of his lips and mirrored the expression. "Of course I remember. My trip with Rhianna and Lord Brighton on their honeymoon to France was not nearly as exciting as it ought to have been after that."

"Because you missed me," he said confidently.

She, of course, would confirm nothing of the sort.

"It was a sweet kiss, was it not?" he reminisced.

"Yes, as it ought to have been. I was twelve, you remember."

"Yes, and now…" Taking her hands, he held her arms out to her sides and looked her over. "…nearly a woman."

"Very nearly," she agreed.

"You haven't let me kiss you much since then."

He pulled her near to him, and she saw desire in his eyes.

"Of course not," she told him sternly. "How else is a girl to keep a *beau* wrapped around her little finger? You should be left always wanting me."

She offered a mischievous grin, knowing all too well the effect her dimples would have upon him, and he lowered his lips to her ear.

"You are cruel to me, Audra Kingsley," he whispered. "The biggest tease there ever was."

Crispin nibbled her earlobe and she laughed. "Lord Crispin, I am as proper a lady as there ever was."

"You are a perfect devil." He kissed along the line of her jaw. "Are you going to tease the other men in London, Audra?"

Leaning into his kisses, she sighed. "Now, why would I do that?"

"Because they would be defenseless against you, and you know it," he breathed, his lips tracing the curve of her neck. "You could have the lot of them wrapped around said little finger."

"My little finger only has room for you," she promised.

Crispin, his hands clasped behind her, pressed his forehead to hers. His brows pulled straight and his eyes narrowed. He lost all humor as a serious expression fell over his face, and with visible effort he steadied his breathing.

"I love you, Audra," he suddenly confessed.

The sound of rapid, fluttering heartbeats tickled her ears, and she was quite unable to distinguish if they were Crispin's, her own, or a combination of the two. Of course he loved her. He may have never before said so, but she knew he loved her, and *had* loved her for four years. And yet there was something powerful in the vocalization of it that struck her speechless, and she marveled at how a belief unuttered became truth when said aloud.

"I know," she returned.

Audra tried to skip away, but only got so far as the swing upon the old oak before finding herself caught between it and her beloved. She sat as Crispin wrapped his fingers around the swing's ropes, entrapping her with his arms so escape was impossible.

Without a word, she tugged on his cravat, undoing it so it fell loosely against his vest. It was a childish thing to do, and she knew it.

If only I were out, she told herself, *then I would know what to do*.

"Tell me you love me," Crispin pleaded. "I know you do, but I want to hear you say it. I dream of it, Audra. I dream of hearing those melodious words fall from your sweet mouth. My heart longs for it, as it longs for you. Please, Audra, I beg it of you."

Audra grew serious. Of course she loved him in return. She had loved him always. Crispin Brighton was the only boy she had ever loved, and she would love him for all time.

Audra rose from the swing's seat. Running the tips of her fingers along a familiar, square jaw, she eased his lips to hers and kissed him gently. A tender peck—it was almost all she ever allowed, and he had never taken advantage.

With her lips still touching his, she opened her eyes and quietly said, "I love you."

She said it as if it were her greatest secret, although, to all who knew her, it was no secret at all. Still as a bird, she watched his lashes separate and his dilated, sky-blue eyes gaze at her longingly. A wide smile crawled across his face as she fell back onto flat feet, his expression beaming and tortured at the same time.

"You can have no idea the agony I live with every day that you are not mine."

"I will be yours," she promised in a quiet voice. "My heart already is."

"Then," he said, reaching into his pocket, "will you take this?" Crispin revealed a chain that held at the end of it a ring, and within the ring a lock of his hair. "Until we can be officially engaged, will you wear it? Wear it as a promise that you will be mine?"

With a gentle nod, she smiled, and he placed it carefully over her curls. Once it hung about her neck, Audra reached for the dangling pendant and clutched it tightly in her palm.

"I will suffer tremendously while you are in London," he told her.

Audra knew she would be equally as wretched, but at once refused to be so until the time came where she must be.

"Come," she invited, pulling him farther into the garden. "I cannot bear to be miserable until it is absolutely unavoidable. Let us enjoy this time we have together."

She doubted her words had the desired effect on him, but he followed her lead, and she determined to keep him to herself until Miss Mauvreen found them, or the dark of evening forced them back to Ravensleigh.

•••

Lady Moira Brighton had not seen her sister, Lady Angela Sutherland, in years. Twenty, in fact, just shortly after Crispin was born. Due only to their dissimilar personalities and Angela's numerous and distant relocations and marriages, it had also been many years since either had even exchanged letters. At the time she wrote to her, Lady Brighton was not even sure of her sister's last name. "Sutherland" was the last she was aware of, but in her younger days Angela had a talent for marrying older gentlemen and seemed a perpetual widow.

Fortunately, when Lady Brighton—with Lord Kingsley's approval—reached out to her and requested her as a sponsor for Audra at court, Angela not only received the letter, but was more than obliging. She was in a carriage on her way to Ravensleigh in a month's time, full of enthusiasm for the task. Having no daughters of her own, she leapt at the chance to take Audra to the Brightons' London townhouse.

"Oh, I just feel so terrible that the girl has no one to take her to St. James," Lady Sutherland told her sister in the Ravensleigh drawing room. "To lose one's mother at such a young age…What was it she died from? Oh! Never mind that. I am very glad you called on me."

Lady Brighton sipped her Earl Gray tea, her own enthusiasm capped only by her own inability to join them on the trip.

"I am delighted she will be going with you. I would have taken her but for the baby. Even though Rhianna and James are doing well, I just cannot imagine leaving them at this time."

Lady Sutherland waved her hand wildly through the air, as if swatting a troublesome gnat. "Oh, no, no, no—certainly not! Your place is here. I will see to it Lady Audra finds herself a fine, suitable husband."

As her sister's expressions revealed her fullest devotion to the project, Lady Brighton laughed. "I admire your enthusiasm, Angela, but I suspect your services *there* will not be needed."

Lady Sutherland looked on her with distinct confusion from opposite a rosewood tea table. "Whatever do you mean?"

Lady Brighton was careful to break the news delicately to her eager sister. "Audra and Crispin have been close these last four years. Her coming out is the only thing that stands in their way."

Lady Sutherland rested her teacup in her lap. "I see."

"I hope that doesn't take too much of the fun out of it for you."

"Oh, no, indeed!" she recovered. "From what you have told me of Lady Audra, Crispin will have done quite well for himself. Is she not heiress to Kingsley Manor?"

"Well, yes," Lady Brighton said, with her usual modesty. "I suppose that does work out, as I am certain Crispin would have married her had she not two pence to her name."

"Ah, young love!"

"I admit, I did not think they would be so devoted these four years. I will be glad to see them settled and, I imagine, happy."

Audra's arrival was announced and she entered the room, a halo of happiness glowing all about her. The ladies rose from their places beside the fireplace, and Lady Brighton introduced them to one another.

"It is a pleasure to make your acquaintance, Lady Audra," said Lady Sutherland, a giddy smile forcing her mouth to twist as if pursing her lips. "My sister has nothing but wonderful things to say about you."

"Lady Sutherland, I am very grateful for your sponsorship," said Audra, taking her hands in an expression of appreciation.

"I understand you are quite ready for your appearance at St. James," said the lady in a tone Lady Brighton thought encompassed all the pride of one who had been a part of the enterprise from the start.

"Oh! Indeed I am, yes. All thanks to your kind sister, of course. My gown is nearly complete. There is only one more fitting to be done, or perhaps two. It is the product of a long-kept promise that she should pick a gown for me when my time came, and it shall double as a wedding dress. Lady Brighton has such wonderful taste. And we have practiced my walking extensively with the tablecloth pinned between my shoulders. I do believe I could walk backwards with an extensive train."

Lady Sutherland nodded approvingly, and with a glance at her sister, said, "It does indeed sound as if you are quite ready, Lady Audra. And what of your curtsey to the queen? Have you practiced that, as well?"

"Indeed, yes! I hope to look quite an expert."

"Well! It does seem to me," said Lady Sutherland, "that once your gown is complete, we ought not to delay. London awaits!"

•••

Guilford, Lord Kingsley, planned a dinner at Kingsley Manor the night before his daughter was to depart for London. He invited the Brighton family, as well as Lady Sutherland, and had a fine spread laid out in the mahogany dining room. Salmon with shrimp sauce, roasted goose and quail with truffles, with accents of peas, turtle soup, mince pie, plum pudding, and breads. A crystal bowl of cherry-cheeked apples, ripe oranges, and pears accented the table beautifully, daring the diners to take a bite.

It was a feast fit for a king, and unsurprisingly Guilford Kingsley showed he would have nothing less with which to send his daughter off to the city of London. The servants had slaved for hours to prepare such a banquet, and all the best silverware had been laid out, knives and forks with mahogany-stained ivory handles, the finest glassware, and the most elegant porcelain graced the table, presenting an impressive yet orderly spread.

"Really, Papa, you did not need to make dinner such a grand affair," Audra told him, stirring her turtle soup and allowing it to cool.

"Oh, pishposh!" cried Guilford. "I ought to have done more, surely. You are my cherished one, my dear Audra. I am very proud of you, and I want to see you well off to London." Turning his attention to his daughter's patroness, he said, "Lady Sutherland, you are very kind to take Audra to St. James, and I have instructed her to be as well-behaved as is in her nature."

"Good heavens," laughed Lady Sutherland, pressing a bejeweled hand to her large bosom, "I am sure that is quite unnecessary. I have no doubt Lady Audra will be quite the lady. The belle of the ball, to be sure."

"Yes, I am sure she will be a perfect mouse," teased Thayne, arousing stifled giggles from those who knew Audra.

Audra laughed, too, but the response was perfunctory, for she had heard hardly a word that was spoken. She had a talent for appearing attentive even when her mind was elsewhere, and at this moment, her mind was on her beloved, who sat across the table, his eyes raking over her devilishly and a smile turning up the sides of his lips.

Audra was not oblivious to her enhanced charms, thanks to a new, cream-and-pink dress that complemented her fair skin and light hair. When she examined herself in the mirror before coming down to the dining room, she admired how the dress highlighted her sapphire eyes among a bouquet of sweet, pastel colors. Upon examining its off-the-shoulder neckline, puffed sleeves, and pink satin sash that accentuated her small waist, with a row of matching pink, satin bows lining the front of her skirt, she found it was very pleasing to her. Audra knew she looked pretty, and she *felt* pretty.

Of course, Crispin always had a way of making her feel so, new dress or not. Neither spoiled an opportunity to meet the other's gaze this night, and Crispin frequently searched her bosom for a sign of the ring he had given her earlier. The chain was long, and she kept it carefully hidden within the fabric of her bodice. Occasionally, she fingered the chain to remind him it was there, as near to her heart as her promise to him.

Crispin was not without his own gestures. At one point, with a simple tug of his ear he reminded her of a moment earlier that evening when he surprised her by catching her earring with his tongue. Holding it captive in his mouth, he followed its wire until his lips were wrapped around her earlobe. The stirrings aroused by the memory took Audra quite unexpectedly, and she was sure her cheeks radiated with a rosy glow. She fiddled with her skirts and glared at her turtle soup while doing battle with the enkindled core of her body. Such desires were new to her, and only recently had she begun to pay them any mind. Now she wondered, if such reactions were the result of his playful yet guarded nibbles, how would she respond when the physical restrictions demanded by their unwed state were lifted? The unladylike thought brought goose bumps to her arms, and she dared wonder to what heights their unrepressed expressions would take them. Of course, she knew she ought to push such thoughts away, but she allowed them to linger and admired her Crispin from across the table without interruption.

And there was great opportunity to appreciate her view of Crispin, as Lady Sutherland commanded the attention of the table. She was fond of recalling her own Presentation Day at court, and was a great one for details—minute details, but remembered with clarity thirty years hence. Those present listened to her patiently and with smiles, even when the lady subjected them to repetitions of broad portions of her experience. Occasionally, Lady Sutherland would break her memoir to either offer a compliment on the house or ask a pointed question about its property or how many servants Lord Kingsley kept, and then without a breath return to her reminiscences.

Crispin's brother, Thayne, seemed by his expression to think Lady Sutherland humorous and silly, and he frequently forced a smirk from his face when she spoke. His wife, Rhianna, offered Audra knowing glances at Lady Sutherland's lengthy rambles and from her seat beside Audra was in an excellent position to remark it fortunate her sister was not to spend more than a fortnight with the excitable woman. Audra agreed with this sentiment. Lady Sutherland was undoubtedly a woman best encountered in small doses—a woman very unlike her sister, Lady Brighton, who was everything that was sensible, calm, and intelligent.

After dinner, when all parties converged into the drawing room, Lady Sutherland fell passionately in love with the grand piano.

"What a fine instrument!" she exclaimed, and was at once adamant that Audra bestow her with a sampling of her talents on the pianoforte.

Audra was not of a shy nature, and having no objections to singing for Lady Sutherland slipped onto the bench.

"It is made finer by its pianist," declared Crispin, sauntering towards her. "May I join you?" he asked Audra.

"You may," she invited.

Crispin slid onto the black bench beside her and stole her hand for a quick kiss. "I envy the keys that have the privilege of having these fingers play upon them."

"Oh, I am sure you have a lovely singing voice, my dear nephew," protested Lady Sutherland abruptly, "but I am so fond of a solo, female voice. Lady Audra, I hope you will indulge me."

Without looking to his aunt, Crispin offered Audra a disappointed yet resigned look, and, running his thumb across her fingers, left to take a seat while Audra obliged. Lady Sutherland was quick to fuss over her natural abilities and proficiency—all while Audra was yet singing. Audra wondered if the lady had, in fact, listened to a note of her song, yet Lady Sutherland applauded her and declared London's young debutantes would most certainly not be able to hold a candle to her.

There was, of course, one person who was paying acute attention, as he always did, and that meant far more to Audra than

Lady Sutherland's inattention. While her fingers danced upon the keys, Crispin looked prouder than her own father, and his chest rose and fell with every note as if the music she produced were the force behind his every breath.

•••

When the time came for the Brighton Family to board their carriage and return to Ravensleigh, Crispin stole Audra away for a private moment near the portico.

"One day," he told her, smiling, "I will have the privilege of beginning and ending my every day looking at this beautiful face."

"One day soon," she replied, "and I shall have the pleasure of seeing the morning whiskers upon yours. I wonder; would you let me shave you?"

"I believe," he said, lowering his voice, "I would let you do a great many things to me."

"Good heavens!" cried Lady Sutherland from the carriage. "Lord Brighton, would you not call your brother to the coach? Lady Audra is going to need her rest, for we have the beginning of a lengthy trip tomorrow morning."

Audra met Thayne's eyes pleadingly. Lady Sutherland might have been enthusiastic to sleep her night away to hurry the morning along, but Audra saw no need of hurrying her and Crispin's goodbyes. Hardly a day in the last four years had passed where they had been apart, and the pressure of separation weighed heavily upon her. Crispin could have said goodbye for hours, and she would not have rushed him away.

"Crispin," Thayne said in a disinterested, drawling voice, "when you're ready."

And with that, Thayne extended his hand for Lady Sutherland to enter the carriage. She pursed her lips at his unhurried remark and with squared shoulders entered the vehicle. Audra giggled at her future brother-in-law's handling of Lady Sutherland, and was grateful for the few extra minutes he bought for them.

In the present company, Audra knew Crispin thought little of pressing his lips to her cheek. He did so lightly, and then ran the tip of his nose along her neck with a long, slow inhale.

"I shall surround myself with the scent of sweet pea until you return," Crispin told her, referring to her regular perfume. "But it shall be only a hollow reminder of you, my love. The scent of your sweet skin at the base will not be there, and that is what I love the best."

Not knowing her own scent, but knowing his well, she knew what he would be missing.

Taking her hands in his and pressing his lips to them, he said, "Come home to me, my love."

"As fast as I can," she promised as he reluctantly dropped her hands and made his way to the carriage.

The others had climbed into the carriage when Crispin placed a foot on the lower, cast iron step and then turned for a final glance at her. Audra pressed her hand to her bodice, where, safely supported by the gold chain and tucked between her breasts, was the promise ring he had given her. Crispin nodded to Lord Kingsley, and the Brighton carriage's wheels began to turn.

Lord Kingsley moved to his daughter's side and placed an arm about her shoulders, and with a sudden, sharp ache, she watched the vehicle turn up the road toward Ravensleigh.

• • •

The next morning, once the carriage was loaded, Audra hurried a kiss to her father's cheek. She waved to him enthusiastically as they departed, thinking that no sooner than she waved goodbye would she be waving hello.

After last night's vision of Crispin leaving Kingsley Manor threatened to rip her heart in two, she had spent a wakeful night considering her options. Either she could leave Thornton with renewed misery, or she could again attempt to look positively on her brief time in London. In the end, she decided it possible to attempt the latter. After all, she had looked forward to this day for so long, Audra determined she owed it to herself to be cheerful. She would be home soon enough.

Chapter Three

The hour was late when they pulled up to the terraced London townhouse on Queen Anne Street. It was too dark to admire the Craigleath stone face, but as they prepared to enter, the delicate Neoclassical moldings in the portico gained Audra's admiration.

While servants rushed to assist with their baggage, Audra removed her gloves and bonnet as she entered the hall. The entry was essentially what she expected of a townhouse. The stone floor was less than impressive compared to the marble of Kingsley Manor, and lacked the pillars that outlined her home's wide, central space. She was surprised to find that not even a chandelier graced the ceiling, leaving the heavy, octagon plaster moldings and ceiling roses with nothing to highlight their beauty but for a single fanlight by day and an oil lamp by night.

The doors to her immediate left and right opened up to the sitting and drawing rooms. These she found pleasantly and lavishly decorated. Indeed, the femininely upholstered chairs and sofas, the pastel ceilings that matched pastel-striped and floral wallpapers, the walls ornamented with fluted cornices and gilt-framed pictures, and the wood-paneled floors bedecked with rich, oriental carpets were cluttered to perfection.

The doorway ahead of her opened up to a plain set of straight, wooden stairs, which she was told led to the first-floor bedrooms, the second-floor study and library, and third-floor attic. The barley twisted balustrades were impressive, but in her mind nothing to the graceful curves of Kingsley Manor's winding, front staircase.

To the left and right of the stairs, one would find a terrace and dining room. Audra managed a peek at the latter before she and Lady Sutherland withdrew to the drawing room for refreshments. The pleasant sight of marble met her in the form of the fireplace surround, and Audra thought it handsomely displayed against crimson-colored walls. The large dining room table still left plenty of room for a games table and sideboard. It was manly, but agreeable.

The travelers' bags were brought in and refreshments immediately offered. The servants seemed out of practice yet anxious to please, their eyes resting heavily upon Audra and Lady Sutherland, as if being found unready in their moment of need was their greatest fear. Audra found herself shifting uncomfortably as the servants stared, and at one point she put down her tea. She met their gazes occasionally, and theirs would fall to the floor as if a heavy weight were at once upon their lashes. And still, turning her attention to Lady Sutherland, who could speak of St. James in the most exhausted of states, Audra would sense the servants' gazes upon her once more. Audra imagined them uncovering the furniture only days before their guests' arrival, the excitement of their coming reason enough for the entire house to billow with excitement. No one but the servants had been at the house in months, and with this mindset, she could excuse them.

After a more thorough examination, the Brightons' nine-hundred-square-foot London townhouse seemed small to her, not because it was any smaller than the surrounding townhouses, but because she was used to large, country estates. And not just any country estates. Kingsley Manor and Ravensleigh were renowned throughout the country for their size and their grandeur—which, of course, was exactly how she liked them.

Audra did not like to think of herself as spoiled. Though she knew it was entirely possible she might be a touch so. She fought this idea vehemently, knowing that, since her mother was not alive to teach her *not* to be spoiled, she had to do the best she could by herself. Her governess, Miss Mauvreen, did try, but her focus fell mostly on taming Audra's outspoken and impetuous personality. Audra soon decided there was no harm in preferring the country to town, and the matter troubled her no further.

She was very pleased with her own bedchamber. It was attractive—exquisite, even. The four-post bed, the frame of a full-length mirror, a writing table, and a Chippendale chair were painted ivory and gold. The light colors gave the bedroom a bright appearance, even though the paintwork was a sea-green, and the same color was embroidered into the quilt, tented bed hangings, and window curtains, with the faintest hint of cherry. She smiled with satisfaction at the sight of it. It was a room she found comfortable and pleasant. A room she could tolerate until she could put London behind her and return home to Crispin.

One of the servant girls rapped on the door. Audra recognized her as Molly, the girl specially in charge of bringing her luggage to her room.

"Come in," Audra invited.

Molly was a quiet thing of about eighteen, the sort of servant who knew so well how to be invisible she hardly knew how to make herself known when required.

"I beg your pardon, Lady Audra, but Lady Brighton sent very specific instructions that you should be given this." And with that, Molly held out a framed baby portrait. "It is Lord Crispin at six months."

"Oh!"

The sight of his sky-blue eyes threw her into a state of such happiness; she thought she might throw her arms around Molly's narrow frame.

"Did you know him?" Audra asked her, cradling the portrait to her bosom.

Molly shook her head. "No, Lady Audra. I've only worked here about a year, and Lord Crispin hasn't come since his levee, I believe. But what a handsome baby, if I may say so. He must be a handsome man."

"Oh, yes," Audra agreed, examining the portrait again in raptures. "Very handsome. I do so hope to have a baby just like him. My sister—that is to say, my future sister-in-law—she just had the most perfect little baby boy…" Audra caught herself from going further. That she so wished to be a mother, and soon, was no doubt something Molly cared little about. "Thank you for this."

Molly nodded and excused herself, leaving Audra to take her time positioning the portrait at just the perfect angle on her dresser.

Once in her bedclothes, Audra sat in the Chippendale chair beside the writing desk and set out to write a letter home confirming their safe arrival in London. Despite the traveling and the late hour, she would not rest until it was ready for the morning's post. In her closing lines, she smiled to herself as she assured her loved ones that she would be home as soon as the presentation process was completed.

•••

St. James Palace, London, March, 1836

A copy of Tuesday's *The London Gazette* was clutched tightly in Lady Angela Sutherland's hands. The instructions were specific:

NOTICE is hereby given, that all carriages coming to Her Majesty's Drawing-Room at St. James's-palace, on Thursday the 24th of March, are to fall to the line at the top of St. James's-street, come down the left hand side of the street, round the corner of Pall-mall, and enter at the iron gate nearest to the Palace, set down at the Arcade, return by the iron gate nearest to Marlborough-house, and pass through Pall-mall into St. James's-square…

The gate at the top of Constitution-hill will be open only for the carriages of persons having the privilege of the entree, which are to proceed down the Park, and enter the Palace at Stable-yard-gate, turn into the Ambassadors'-court, set down at the Arcade, and go out into Cleveland-row…

Lady Sutherland read these guidelines over and over again, both to herself and aloud. To say she was excited as their carriage arrived at St. James Palace would be a severe understatement. To Audra, she seemed to be reliving her own Presentation Day experience of many years ago, and the eccentricity previously revealed in Lady Sutherland magnified itself. Repeatedly, she reminded Audra to hold her shoulders back, to hold her flower just so—and where were her three official name cards again?

"Lest you forget, Lady Audra, you will need *one* to be left in the Anti-room, *another* for the Lord in Waiting to the King, and *one* for the Lord Chamberlain to give to the Queen…"

Though her voice rose to a shrill level at the word "Queen," her escalated enthusiasm did not annoy Audra as it might have annoyed other girls. Audra's personality was such that she was able to see the good intentions of a woman willing to sponsor a girl known to her only as a friend of her all-but-estranged sister. Indeed, Audra's own gratefulness for the sponsorship more than allowed her to overlook any emotional overindulgence on the part of the lady.

Not to mention, Audra's level of stress on Presentation Day was not that of other girls, either. While, certainly, she was rightly concerned with tripping over her train or losing her feathers, Presentation Day for her was where the stress began and ended. The others would go on to balls and dinners and look for *beaus* at the theater in hopes of catching a decent husband. But Audra would have none of that. She would return to Thornton without a care in the world and marry her one and only love. Under such circumstances, there was really no irritant strong enough to dampen her spirits or otherwise alter her happy mood.

From Ambassadors' Court, they soon made their way among the excitable crowds to the north-facing main gate in the Clock Tower. With a brisk walk, Lady Sutherland led Audra along the colonnade in Colour Court to Wren's Grand Staircase, which led to the Armory and Tapestry rooms. Once there, Audra caught her breath as Lady Sutherland explained—again—that it was there her credentials would be examined before she could gain entry to the Queen Anne Room, and there, also, that they would wait.

The rooms were hot and overcrowded with young debutantes and their sponsors. Audra regretted that she carried a flower and not a fan, as the latter would have served a greater purpose in the airless rooms. Before them stood two doors that led to the Presence Chamber—and Queen Adelaide. Soon, Audra would be called to enter, and no sooner than she did so, the whole thing would be done with.

She watched and grew very nervous as one girl after another was called to enter, their trains spread out by gentlemen in waiting before the doors closed behind them. They each returned the way they entered, smiles beaming across their perspiring faces, a few wiping clammy hands on their hoop skirts once safely returned from the Queen Anne Room.

Audra smoothed the skirts of her own white dress that had been created for her under Lady Brighton's gifted oversight. The lady who would be her mother-in-law had taken her for all the fittings and helped her choose all the correct accessories of jewelry and slippers. The pale pink train, when let down, would be covered by a floating veil, its origin a tulle headdress ornamented with the required white feathers. She was very fond of it, but much too anxious to give it two thoughts now.

"Lady Audra."

She started at the call of her name. Audra cast Lady Sutherland a blissful parting glance before approaching the door pointed out to her. Then, her train was spread and the double doors opened to her. A moment later, and she was gliding toward the presence of the Queen, her dress with its effusion of fabrics gracefully sweeping the floor around her.

The approach to the Throne Room was farther than she had imagined, and it was one of only two things she would clearly remember when the whole experience was complete. The other was a blur of red, white, and gold that swathed the walls, doors, floor, and ceiling. Fear seized her as she peered from the Queen Anne Room to the Entrée Room to the Throne, where sat Queen Adelaide.

Only just as suddenly, calm replaced the fear, and Audra allowed a daydream—indeed, a glimpse of the future—to play out before her eyes. And with one blink, the Queen was not what Audra saw before her. Of course, the Queen was *there*, but what she saw was Crispin. Audra took her steps bravely, at once walking toward *him*, her groom, and she, his bride, and she marched effortlessly toward the altar. The vividness of this happy dream was such that Audra was entirely unaware not only of the monarch, but the great room, as well as the group of royalties in their showy gowns and uniforms.

"Lady Audra Kingsley."

At this second announcement of her name, Audra instinctively dropped into the graceful, full-court curtsey she had so diligently practiced. Then, as Audra was the daughter of a peer, the Queen kissed her forehead. Audra curtseyed again to the Queen, then to the royalties. A gentleman in waiting placed her train back over her arm, and she backed her way seamlessly out of the State Apartments.

And with that short ceremony, Audra Kingsley returned to the Tapestry Room a full-fledged member of Society, and it was now that her engagement to Crispin could at long last become official.

• • •

"Pardon me," said a gentle-voiced, brown-haired debutante. She knelt to the floor, white skirts ballooning around her, and lifted something from Audra's feet. One of her feathers fluttered beside her as she rose. "Did you drop this note?"

Audra, searching eagerly for Lady Sutherland, who had gone missing among the crowd, almost entirely ignored the outstretched hand of the girl beside her. "No, I don't think so, but thank you."

"Certainly." Turning to two other debutantes, Audra overheard the same girl ask, "Are either of you Lady Audra Kingsley?"

Audra turned sharply to the sound of her name. "I beg your pardon?"

The brown-haired girl looked puzzled at Audra's quick response. Her eyes fell to the note, and she held it out to Audra a second time. Scribbled blotchily in black ink were the words "Lady Audra Kingsley."

"Do you know her?" the brown-haired girl asked.

"There you are!" waved Lady Sutherland, while pushing her way through the crowd toward Audra.

"Yes," Audra said abruptly, and she took the note and stuffed it quickly into her glove.

"Congratulations, darling," said Lady Sutherland, placing her hands about her shoulders. "How does it feel to be a woman in Society?"

"It feels wonderful," said Audra, brimming with happiness.

"Miss DeBlock, how nice to see you," said Lady Sutherland, turning to the brunette girl standing beside Audra. "Have you met Lady Audra Kingsley?" The girls curtseyed to each other. "This is Miss Embeth DeBlock, daughter of my acquaintance, Lady DeBlock of York. Miss DeBlock, I was just speaking with your mother, and it appears congratulations are in order."

"Yes, indeed, Lady Sutherland."

Embeth was giddy, yet calm compared with many of the other debutantes. Her eyebrows were lifted high above dancing eyes, and her round cheeks bubbled when her lips parted into a wide, toothy smile. The girl's mother found their group. Audra was introduced, and Lady DeBlock chatted momentarily with Lady Sutherland.

"Are you applying for a subscription to Almack's?" she overheard Lady DeBlock asking.

"Oh, indeed, yes," said Lady Sutherland, bursting at the very mention of Almack's.

The confirmation caught Audra off-guard and she felt an inclination to turn her head in Lady Sutherland's direction. Audra had supposed just a single night would be applied for, as even a set would have been more balls than she would be around to attend. After a moment's consideration, however, she allowed it was Lady Sutherland's excitement that left the specifics out of the conversation and dismissed any concerns over the subject.

"Pending the decisions of the Ladies of the Committee, perhaps we shall see each other at Almack's," said Embeth to Audra, hopefulness in her voice.

"Oh, no need to wait until then," said Lady Sutherland. "Why do we not plan to go riding in Hyde Park together tomorrow?"

Audra saw little point in making friends when her time in London was so limited, but Embeth DeBlock had a kind sweetness in her face, and Audra liked her. Besides, there might as well be someone to look forward to seeing as long as she was in town, and Audra quickly shared the group's hopes of riding along Rotten Row the following day.

• • •

Audra shut the door to her bedroom with the intention of making her way to the ivory-and-gold secretary to write a letter to Lady

Brighton of the day's events. As she walked and began to remove her gloves, a letter addressed to "Lady Audra Kingsley" fluttered to the oriental rug, stopping her in her tracks. She had forgotten all about its appearance at St. James, and how she had hidden it. She hardly knew why she hid it, except that its mysterious nature seemed to require that she do so.

Audra lifted her skirts to kneel beside it and held it over her lap. She wasted no time in opening it now, and read the following words:

> Dear Lady Audra,
> It was an unfathomable privilege to rest my eyes upon you when you arrived in St. James Square today. You are a heavenly creature, and you cannot imagine my happiness in discovering you may be at Almack's, as will I. I look forward to the time when I am blessed with the indulgence of seeing you again. Until then—
> I am & co,
> Your Secret Admirer

Chapter Four

Audra soon discovered that any suggestion of being denied acceptance to Almack's threw Lady Sutherland into hysterics, and she was forced to keep the vulgar thoughts to herself. Audra, for her part, was already several days into her London excursion, and despite the charms of riding in Hyde Park, the fun of shopping on Bond and Regent Streets, the joys of the operas of Covent Garden, and the pleasurable company of Embeth DeBlock and her mother, she was quite ready to go home. As it was, her coming out ball at Almack's was the final matter standing between her and Crispin, and Audra easily decided in her heart that, should the six reigning lady patronesses reject her application, she would not be at all disappointed.

On Monday, however, Lady Sutherland was released of her anxiety over the matter. The Countess of Jersey, the Marchioness of Londonderry, Lady Cowper, the Countess of Brownlow, Lady Willoughby D'Eresby, and the Countess of Euston, all of them familiar with Audra's father, Guilford, Lord Kingsley, embraced Audra with open arms. Lady Sutherland was not a particular favorite of theirs, but since she was a previous member of Almack's, and a willing subject of ridicule for them, they consented to her presence as Audra's patroness. Lady Sutherland positively glowed as a voucher for a full subscription was provided to her by Almack's owner, Mr. Willis.

On Wednesday, Almack's doors opened at ten o'clock in the evening, and the commotion was unlike anything Audra could have envisioned. Even the most elaborate of Kingsley Manor's balls that she had watched from afar had not seen the like, as an attendance of over five hundred made their way to the unassuming Palladian building on King's Street. When Audra had stepped down from her carriage, she caught a brief glimpse of the others lining up behind her, and she started at the hallooing of coachmen and footmen who were doing their best to maintain order and keep the crowds in motion. She had never been surrounded by so many people in all her life, and the excitement that exuded from them was infectious. As she and Lady Sutherland were ushered through the doors, a little thrill found its way through her body.

At eleven o'clock, John Weippert struck up his band on the orchestra balcony of Almack's large room. At once, the debutantes swirled along the polished, roped-off dance floor, a collective sea of corkscrew curls and braided buns. Girls freshly introduced to society danced the waltz and gallopade with square-shouldered gentleman who twirled their ladies gracefully while sneaking sideways glances at girls prettier than their partners.

The excitement and newness of the experience lasted only a short while for Audra until the flushed faces, the wide smiles, and the eagerness in the expressions of the girls around her struck a sharp chord. Hearts impatient to fall in love filled the crowd, and despite any thrill she had felt upon first entering the establishment, an overwhelming sensation of isolation now came over her. It was so sudden it stopped her breath, and the realization she did not belong sat heavy upon her breast.

She had hoped to enjoy her coming out appearance before becoming a married woman. She had dreamed of this day since before she could remember. But the phantasm of enjoyment vaporized without a trace, and she was left with the knowledge that it simply had never been there. Despite the wonders of the famed establishment where she now found herself, her heart was not in it. And how could it have been? Her heart had not only been claimed by another, but it had never followed her to London.

No, she realized at once that her heart lived apart from her, with Crispin, and she felt only a fragment of herself.

In an instant, Audra longed to be whole again, to collect the pieces of herself that had scattered along the roads on her way to the city. And she knew there was only one thing to be done. She must return home to Thornton as soon as possible. Oh, that she could speed up this night! How she wished for tomorrow to come!

The dancing partner the Ladies of the Committee had chosen for Audra for her first set, a man considered a great catch to the *ton*, won Audra the envy of almost every other female in the room. She, of course, found him less than interesting and rather high strung over the new crowd of females. In fact, his lack of conversation skills and excitable nature was draining to the point that the effects of spending an hour with him were felt long after he was gone. By the time she danced with her second partner, a man equally energized, she was mentally exhausted, and by the third she was certain if she had to engage another such one in conversation she would scream. At the earliest part of the evening she was friendly to them, even charming. But as the hours passed, and fresh understanding of her alienated situation overcame her, the whole night turned thoroughly sour, and when Lady Jersey introduced a gentleman by the name of Lord Everton, Audra cared not a wink to know him, and she very nearly forgot his name.

Prompted by the ever-present, ever-irksome sense of propriety, she managed a disingenuous smile. Audra knew how to fake politeness when required, though she was not fond of the practice. Had her acquaintance with Lord Everton been above even an hour, she might not have pulled it off quite so eloquently. However, preferring numbness to the maddening frustration that had begun to crawl through her from the inside out, she shunned all feelings. After all, her ability to thrust emotion aside until unpleasantness had passed was one of her greatest gifts.

Audra scratched at the pins in her too-tight bun and turned her attention to the gentleman, aged somewhere in his late thirties. He was tall, with wavy, almond-colored hair and chocolate-colored eyes. He had a confident, graceful way about him, and she appreciated his quiet manner. Indeed, she felt less inclined to carrying out a feigned faint to escape the assembly room—an idea she knew she must abandon regardless. At the very thought Audra stifled a laugh, and she had no doubt she would fail to pull off a convincing performance. One had to be serious to be a good actress. And Audra had had quite her fill of seriousness for one week.

"A pleasure to meet you," he said.

Audra forced a gracious reply and, accepting his hand for a waltz, allowed him to lead her onto the floor. He did so with a pleasant smile, and she felt as comfortable as she could in another man's embrace. In fact, she knew not why, but Audra fell quickly at ease with him, and she just as quickly forgot that there was no telling what she might say when she was at ease.

"How old are you?" she asked, not long into their dance.

Audra stunned herself with the question, and one hand flew to her open mouth. Had she, Audra Kingsley, daughter of Guilford, Lord Kingsley, asked such a thing? Horror seeped into her veins and crawled through her, warming her blood and bringing a hot flush to her cheeks.

Lord Everton chuckled. "I am thirty-eight," he confessed, with little hesitation.

His words had an air of amusement and no hint of offense, though he peered at her curiously and said nothing further.

"Well, that must be why," she blurted, feeling she owed him an explanation, and at once realizing this obscure comment offered him none.

Eyeing her with a cocky smile, he returned, "That must be why what?"

"You're not as excitable as the others," she told him. She explained as quickly as it became clear to her. "It makes it much easier to be around you."

"The *others*?" he repeated, maintaining an entertained expression.

"The younger men."

Again, her mouth dropped, but she did not cover it with her hand.

Lord Everton nodded and cocked his head to the side, an ever-present smile pulling widely across his face. "Well, thank you."

"I don't think you're *old*," she told him, hurriedly, "even if you *are* twenty-two years my senior."

At this, Lord Everton laughed aloud, a booming chuckle that drew the attention of the nearby dancers. "Well, you are no bore, Lady Audra."

"Oh! I have dug myself into a ditch, haven't I? I'm so sorry."

"Don't apologize to me, I beg it of you. This is the most fun I've had all evening."

"Are you quite sure I haven't forever offended you?"

As they rose and fell with the dance, he assured her, "Not in the least, my lady. Though I suppose I ought to be mad at you for a short while. Perhaps not talk to you for a good majority of the evening, but I doubt I could bring myself to do it."

Audra flashed him a smile—a genuine one this time. "I'm so glad. I quite like you."

"I am glad of it. I quite like you, as well, but I think I'll lead the conversation for a bit." Looking upward, as if searching for a new subject in the crystals of the chandelier above them, he asked, "Tell me, how do you enjoy the city, Lady Audra?"

She accepted this new topic with pleasure, and when he lowered his brown eyes back to hers, she said, "London has its purposes, but I rather miss home."

"London does have its purposes," he agreed. "Pray, what is its purpose to you?"

She was hoping he would ask where "home" was, as that was the more agreeable subject, and sighed. "I was presented at court."

He twirled her; rather wildly she thought, and on her return told her, "Well, then, welcome to the game."

"I don't intend to play any *game*," she told him, curtly, and at once annoyed. "And what of you, Lord Everton? Does London suit your purposes?"

"Ah," he said, leading her with flowing movements along the slippery floor, "I expect it will. I have been informed by my less tactful female relatives that it is high time I find myself a wife. I've come to suspect they're right, and hope to return home with one."

His honesty amused her, though the way he spoke of wives left something to be desired. The impression he gave when he talked of returning home with one made it sound as if he intended to return home with a new dress coat.

"A serious business, to be sure," Audra said, "though the way you say it, it would seem any woman who agrees to the position would do."

He grinned. "While I believe that to be essentially true, I do have my preferences."

"*Essentially true?*" she repeated. "Are you suggesting it does not matter to you at all whom you marry?"

His was an unreadable expression. "I believe that any man and woman of similar tempers and position in society could certainly make good work of it, and don't see at all why the institution shouldn't work just as well with one woman as with any. Though, as I said, I have my preferences."

Audra's eyebrows were raised high, and though she found his opinions on this subject ridiculous, she liked his candor. And whether he intended it or not, she now found great humor in the dialogue.

"Preferences? Well, pray tell, Lord Everton."

He shrugged, nonchalantly. "I am particularly drawn to blonde hair and blue eyes."

This description of her own features was not lost on Audra as Lord Everton gazed into her eyes with great exaggeration.

"For heaven's sake!" she cried. "Lord Everton, do not look at me like that!"

"I can see you would be a difficult lady to win over," he said, his smiling lips twisting to one side.

"Do not look at me as a challenge, Lord Everton. I have my own plans; it is only fair for you to know. In fact, I am an engaged woman."

"Engaged?" he repeated, disbelief laced through his voice. "So soon after your presentation at court? I daresay, that must be a record."

"I beg your pardon," she said, "but you don't know what you're talking about."

He nodded with a thoughtful air. "Officially engaged?" he asked.

Officially.

The word lingered in the air between them for a moment. Audra struggled inwardly, yet despite considerable efforts, it seemed nothing resembling what she wanted to say could be formed into a sentence.

Lord Everton circled her gracefully to Bach. "The way I see it, Lady Audra, there is only one type of engagement. Either you *are* or you *aren't*. Now, indulge me with an answer to my question. Are you an officially engaged woman?"

Audra bit the inside of her cheek to keep from snapping at him. "I will be," she told him, tersely, "the second I get home. Now, will you stop with that grin?"

"As you wish, Lady Audra." Lord Everton contorted his face to a mock expression of seriousness. "He is a fortunate fellow," he openly lamented. "If only…"

"If only *what?*" she said.

"If only I could change your mind."

A smile, stiff and unwilling, crawled across her face. Lord Everton was nothing if not straightforward. And Audra loved people who were straightforward.

"Well, you can't," she told him flatly, "so don't bother."

Barely did she finish her sentence when the song drew to a close, and the audience erupted with applause. Audra and Lord Everton joined in, and then prepared to part.

"I hope you find what you are looking for," she told him with a curtsey.

He bowed. "If I may, it was a delight to stand up with you, Lady Audra. I hope you will do me the honor again."

"As I am sure my patroness will not leave Almack's until the band plays 'God Save The Queen,' I would welcome the distraction, Lord Everton."

"I am glad to hear you find me distracting."

"I daresay, you are impossible," she told him.

"Upon our next meeting, I hope you will find me impossibly distracting."

Audra took her leave of him with a smile. Anyone who could divert her attention from the ache of not being with Crispin, even if only for a few moments, was a welcomed friend.

...

In February, a portion of the London and Greenwich Railway had opened between Spa Road in Bermondsey and Deptford. There were a number of significant things connected with this event, but only one of them was being discussed this night. It may very well have been the first passenger line to have a terminus in the capital and, where it crossed Deptford Creek, may have proved to be the first example of an elevated railway, but it was the accident that had people at Almack's talking.

Only a few weeks prior, on March seventh, a man named Daniel Holmes, showing himself in no hurry to leave the tracks for the landing, was gruesomely run over and mortally wounded. That others in the immediate area were also wounded did not play a large part in the telling and retelling of the tragic event amongst the evening's company. Audra listened intermittently to the ladies' comments.

"The engine driver, Mr. Millender, drove right into the southbound train," said one.

"As I heard," said another, "he was distracted by Mr. Holmes, who refused to leave the track."

"The whole thing is madness!" cried another. "Mr. Holmes must have been quite out of his mind."

"I understand the runaway engine ran him right over," said her neighbor. "How very gruesome!"

"I was told," said Lady Sutherland, "the London and Greenwich Railroad Resident Director, Mr. Walker, witnessed the tragic event himself, and declared afterwards they have had immense difficulties keeping people away from the tracks."

"I shall certainly never ride a train!" cried the first.

Audra cared not to participate and kept her contrasting opinions to herself, as she thought trains quite fascinating and did not feel a single accident would keep her from riding one, had she the opportunity.

Lady Sutherland continued to talk a good deal about the unfortunate incident and the loathsome trains until she had nothing new to add. At last, Audra got the sense that Lady Sutherland's contemporaries had nothing new to add, either, and she took advantage of the opportunity to glance discreetly at a nearby grandfather clock for the time.

Audra was famished. She had not eaten since breakfast, and even the meager fare of flat toast, dried cake, and sour lemonade at Almack's was highly appealing. Soon, they made their way to one of the tearooms. Audra was pleased to find Embeth DeBlock already there, and she sat with her. It had proved convenient to have an acquaintance with whom she could be on more informal, relaxed terms. Embeth was quiet, and her excitement over Almack's and the Season was reserved compared to most. A wild, giddy girl would have been largely intolerable; Audra had her fill of wild giddiness in Lady Sutherland and was glad when her patroness found conversation at another table.

"Isn't Almack's just splendid?" Embeth remarked as Audra buttered a thin piece of bread. "I can hardly believe I am here at last! Have you not always dreamed of dancing at Almack's?"

"Yes," she managed, feeling it best to keep it to herself that she had grown out of such childhood dreams, and cared not one whit that she was now there.

"Lady Audra, may I tell you a secret?" Embeth asked sheepishly. "I could never tell Mother. She would just die!"

Now, *this* was interesting, and had the potential to keep her distracted for a time. Audra welcomed the suggestion.

"I wish you would!" she told her. "I love secrets. And, please, do call me Audra, because I'm going to call you Embeth."

"Very well." Embeth pressed her lips together and looked about her as if a spy were certainly behind her, listening. "I danced twice with Lord Robert Wesley, and—have you met him?"

Audra vaguely recalled a freckle-faced, lanky sort of boy, with whom she danced her second or third dance of the evening. "I believe so."

Embeth's cheeks flushed crimson. "Well," she went on, "after I stood up with him the second time, and the dance concluded, he confided to me…Oh! I can hardly say it aloud."

"Good gracious, Embeth, go on!"

Her eyes flickered to Audra. "You won't repeat it, will you?"

"Heavens, no!"

"Oh, Audra, it's so…. He said…he said, 'Miss DeBlock, I wish for all the world I could stand up with you *a third time*.'"

She rushed her napkin to her mouth and covered it as a wide smile broke across her face, and her gaze fell to the untouched plate before her. "Can you imagine?" she asked, flustered, barely able to remove the napkin to ask the question.

Audra would have liked Embeth to have said it was one of the other men, the ones with reputations, the ones whose names preceded them, and who were handsome. Embeth was a pretty girl with a large dowry, and Audra thought she could get any one of them.

"He is not particularly…"

Audra stopped. Who was she to say what Embeth should and should not consider handsome?

"I know what you are thinking," Embeth told her, "and, I daresay, Lord Wesley's appearance may not have women clinging to his every extremity. But, you know, my father was a rake. My two brothers were rakes. When I saw the misery they caused my mother and my sisters-in-law, I knew a nice, loyal husband was my goal."

At this, Embeth's captivation with Lord Wesley drew a deeper respect from Audra. "That was sweet of Lord Wesley to want to stand up with you a third time," she replied. "So, you like him?"

"Oh! Yes. He has been so kind and gentlemanly. I do like him." Embeth took a hurried sip of her lemonade. "What about you, Audra? Have you met anyone particularly nice?"

"I am not here to meet anyone particularly nice. I want to go home."

Embeth seemed taken aback, and Audra did not doubt it was her words, more than her tone.

"Is London not to your liking? Are you homesick?" Embeth asked feelingly.

Audra nodded at this last. "Homesick, yes. I am to be married back home. My father encouraged me to come to London to be presented, but at home my engagement can now be made official."

"Oh!" Embeth gave a single hop of excitement. "Congratulations! I can see now why you would have no further business here."

Audra glanced around the room and noted the fluttering eyelashes and flirtatious laughter of the debutantes, and the men clustering about them. The richest girls had the most men beside them, with both the wealthiest and the least wealthy at their sides. Men with more modest fortunes found girls of equal or lesser fortunes, and all were in high spirits.

"No business whatsoever," Audra echoed. She rolled her shoulders to try to release some of the sudden tension.

"I hope to leave London with similar plans," Embeth told her. "I have twin sisters just a year younger than me who are anxious to be presented. I don't want to hold them up." She sighed. "It would be nice to fall in love. Do you love this fellow back in your town of Thornton?"

Audra smiled as Crispin's face appeared in her mind's eyes. "Since we were very young."

"How wonderful!"

"Yes." Audra drifted off with thoughts of her beloved. "He is wonderful."

•••

Toward the end of the evening, Audra danced her second time with Lord Everton. Again, she fell quickly at ease with him, and he did not flirt with her—much. He was fond of twirling her more quickly than the dance required, and just as their dance concluded, a strand of hair fell from its pins. He seemed proud of himself, and she shook her head. He was as pleasant as ever, and she wished him every success in finding himself a suitable wife.

"Was that Lord Everton tossing you about?" asked Lady Sutherland, smiling as Audra approached her. "What a funny fellow!"

Certainly, there was no one in the whole of Almack's who was enjoying themselves as much as Lady Sutherland. No debutante, no hopeful mother, no gentleman amidst the fresh blood in the assembly rooms could match her consummate and inexhaustible high spirits. Audra wondered if the fervent gaiety of the older women surrounding her, while not equal to the matchless happiness of her patroness, was enough to make Lady Sutherland tolerable to them.

Before Audra could make any reply, her patroness went on, "Whatever has happened to your hair, child?"

Lady Sutherland seemed about to leap from her chair, but Audra rested a calming hand over hers. "Not to worry, Lady Sutherland. It is only a runaway curl. I beg you will not disturb yourself and your friends. I suspect with the assistance of a mirror and a new pin I shall be more than equipped to return it to its place. Do enjoy yourself."

This last was an unnecessary suggestion. As Audra reached for her reticule, Lady Sutherland nodded and settled herself more fixedly in her seat, as her immutable joy emanated from her core with a burning glow that would rouse the envy of any hearth.

Audra took leave of her patroness for the nearest mirror. Finding one on the far wall, she placed her feather-trimmed reticule on the table and undid the ribbon drawstrings. Attempting to hold the rogue curl in place, she reached with her free hand for the extra hairpins she packed at the house and felt something crinkle against her fingertips. Her gaze dropped to a folded piece of paper between her linen handkerchief and her calling card case. The loose curl was quickly forgotten as she lifted the document curiously and opened the folds of a hand-written note.

Dear Lady Audra…

Audra's mouth fell, and she instinctively looked about her. If someone had been hoping she would discover it sooner rather than later, they certainly were not waiting around to watch her read it. The fluid movements of the crowd continued without any care to Audra Kingsley or the contents of her reticule. Turning her back to the crowd once more, she held the note low and quickly scanned its contents.

Dear Lady Audra,

While it would, indeed, be easier to gain an introduction by a mutual acquaintance and beg a spot on your dance card, it would not be nearly as fun. Other gentleman may be so dull, but I wish to gain fair lady's interest by avoiding all the usual routes. It is my hope you will find my unconventional note intriguing, and the mystery places me in your favor. You may expect to hear from me again, and soon. I only hope to find myself in your thoughts until then.

Your Secret Admirer

Audra quickly placed the letter back whence it came, even going so far as to rearrange her items in order to place a tin of breath mints over it to bury it further. It was flattering, certainly, and she briefly considered that it was a shame she would not be in London long enough to find out who Secret Admirer was. If only he had revealed himself to her, she could have thanked him for the compliment of his letters, but informed him she was engaged to another and wished him well.

Through the mirror, Audra saw Embeth DeBlock approaching. Swiftly pinning her hair, she turned to meet her. They exchanged bittersweet goodbyes. Audra had enjoyed her company in between dances, and hoped to keep in touch with her. Of course, Audra's return to Thornton was first and foremost in her mind, but she had a lovely foregleam of Embeth and Lord Wesley coming to visit her and Crispin at Kingsley Manor.

Chapter Five

Lady Moira Brighton smiled at Remford as he handed her a letter. "It is from Lady Sutherland," she announced to the breakfast table.

The comment drew the interest of all members of the Brighton family present in Ravensleigh's morning room, but Crispin was certain their hearts did not leap in their breasts as his did. For him, it was almost impossible to remain still while his mother unfolded the letter with slow, calm fingers. Oh! That he could snatch it from her hands! He watched her gaze as it fell on the page, and she read its contents silently to herself. He studied the soft pull of her mouth as she smiled at its words and the deepening of the wrinkles around her eyes as the smile reached them.

"They have arrived safely in London," she announced, pressing one hand lightly over her breast.

Thayne and Rhianna waited silently for her next words with a patience that plucked Crispin's nerve strings. How could they be so still? Even their attention seemed torn, as they smiled at the hiccupping James, whom Thayne rocked gently in his arms. Crispin wanted them out of his peripheral vision and leaned forward. He laid his elbows carelessly on the table and hung on his mother's slightest changes in expression.

"Audra's presentation went beautifully," Lady Brighton continued, her pink lips—not as full as they once were in her youth, but full nonetheless—pulled across a row of gleaming white teeth, "and she was accepted to Almack's for her coming out ball."

Powerful emotions filled Crispin's body, and the combination of them made it almost impossible to decipher one from the other. Jealousy, certainly, of the men who had undoubtedly met her there and held her in their arms, their bodies swaying with hers to the sound of the orchestra; anxiety that she might have enjoyed herself in their company, as one after another of the wealthy, eligible first sons of England's elite families were introduced to her; and impatience for her to return to Thornton, and to him.

The happiness this last seemed to bring to his sister-in-law, Rhianna, did not assist him. He clutched the edge of the table as she declared the St. James and Almack's events "wonderful" and "enchanting" and "exciting." Normally, he liked her very much. But at this moment, not at all, and he was at once finished with his breakfast. Restlessly, he pushed himself away from the table, resting his hands upon his thighs.

The change in Lady Brighton's expression was subtle, but as her brows pulled together ever so slightly, and her eyes narrowed, and her smile lessened, Crispin leapt to the height of alertness.

"What?" he asked.

The word was quick, to the point, and he made sure his tone demanded a quick, to-the-point response.

His mother's gaze flickered to his and then returned to the letter. It appeared she was re-reading its contents to be sure of them before sharing them aloud.

"*What?*" he asked again, choking on the word, his inflection alerting the whole table to his conviction that something was wrong. He was leaning forward again, with no recollection as to when he did so or how his fist had come to rest beside his plate.

Lady Brighton stole another glance at her son and shook her head before continuing. "It says they look forward to spending the Season in London."

Crispin flew to his feet and was at once beside her. Lady Brighton offered him the letter, and he skimmed its contents frantically for this announcement. Even as he read the lines with his own eyes, he made little sense of it.

"…she has made quick friends, and is having such a marvelous time. I adore her so, and can never thank you enough for thinking to call upon me for the service or Lord Sutherland for agreeing to spare me for the Season…"

"I don't understand," he muttered, despairingly.

Sensing their eyes on him, Crispin met each of their glances, hoping someone would fully comprehend Lady Sutherland's meaning and explain it to him. But all he found were expressions of similar bewilderment and—worse—of sympathy.

"Are there no lines from Audra directly?" Rhianna asked.

Crispin knew the answer, but looked the letter over frantically, hoping some might appear. When no such expressions materialized, he shook his head no.

"Brother," said Thayne, encouragingly, "you yourself have been to London. You are aware of how it bustles with people and activity. Audra is a curious girl who has never before seen the like…"

Crispin raised a hand for Thayne to stop speaking. Dropping the letter to the table beside his mother, he turned and exited the room.

•••

As Thayne followed him out of the morning room, and also out of the house, Crispin ignored him. At least, since his older brother was determined to chase after him, Thayne had not attempted conversation.

At Ravensleigh's stables, Crispin saddled up his own horse, and, through the corner of his eye, he watched Thayne do the same. And when he rode out from the stables into the wide-open fields of the family property, his brother followed wordlessly behind.

With the distance Thayne kept between them, Crispin soon forgot his brother was following him at all. He rode along in a fog, the natural world around him seeming a ways off, and he in an airless void, far removed from it. If he'd had any liquor, he would have thought himself drunk—a state he intended to find himself in immediately upon returning to the house. Distortion was strong in his vision, the gray, English skies looking both close and untouchable, the green grass below him both expansive and suffocating. He saw himself in the world, and yet felt a detached spectator of it, both physically and emotionally.

Crispin knew not how long he rode through the open fields. He knew only that, at last, he reined in his horse at the old oak at the back of the house. It was here one of his last, private outings with Audra had taken place, and it was here he could best remember her promise to him—indeed, *hear* her promise to him.

"I see no reason to stay in London once I am presented," she had said. *"I have every intention of coming home as soon as the whole business is done with."*

He had relished these words, draped them around his torso like a blanket, and warmed himself with them in the days after she left. He drew comfort in her assurances, cast his uncertainty aside, and believed her.

"How do you know you will not fall in love with London and want to stay longer?" he had asked.

"Because you are not in London."

He groaned at the memory, even more as he remembered her standing tip-toed against him, her mouth against his, and a confession of love dripping from her lips.

Thayne was now beside him, strong, silent, and supportive.

"Do you think she's met someone?" Crispin asked, glaring at the old oak. "Someone who has more than just a title? A first son?"

Thayne did not hurry a response. Crispin cast him a sidelong glance, and he seemed to think the question over carefully. His brother would not offer him false comfort for the sake of immediate and temporary relief.

"You have been everything to her for years," Thayne told him at last. "No. I have an easier time seeing her enjoying the excitement of a city."

"It's a terrible feeling," Crispin told him, "falling from first place. Going from being everything to…to who knows what."

"Crispin…"

"She said she would come right back. She said the second it was over there was no reason to stay. And now, *she has made quick friends, and is having such a marvelous time*?" He shook his head, recalling the contents of Lady Sutherland's letter. "It just doesn't make any sense. It feels *wrong*." A short silence fell between them before he suddenly announced, "I have to go to London."

"And do what?"

"Talk to her."

"You mean demand she return home with you."

"No," Crispin told him. "I just want to hear it from Audra. I need *her* to tell me she wants to stay."

This much, Thayne seemed to understand. "Why do you not allow Mother to respond to Lady Sutherland? She will write of our surprise and ask for more details. See what the response is before you go galloping to London." Crispin considered this as Thayne added, "What is more, a letter from Lady Audra will likely show up at any moment. Knowing her as I do—as we all do—I cannot imagine she will not write to us directly."

The arrangement was tolerable, albeit barely, and at length, Crispin settled on this course of action. He believed, as his brother said, that Audra would, indeed, write a letter herself. Once her own hand told him it was her desire to remain in London, he could begin to process her wishes.

Until then, he would remain in limbo.

...

When the days passed, and no letter from Audra arrived, no words could console Crispin. The family made efforts to soothe him as he sat for long hours in their midst in pitiful silence, but they did not know he had completely shut himself down to the emotional assistance. He was deeply unhappy, and he wanted to be so. Under such miserable circumstances, he saw no reason to feel otherwise.

Crispin did not assist himself during the nighttime hours, which proved equally long and solitary. In his isolation, his mind wandered freely and without disturbance, the pictures conjured—of Audra, bubbling with gaiety and flirting mercilessly in the ballrooms and theaters of London—making him ill as no illness had touched him before.

One night, with the hours lingering and Crispin in a state of agony unknown to him all the previous days of his life, he shot up in bed and stared into the blackness. And in that blackness, he looked clearly into Audra's youthful face, the setting sun behind her casting a golden radiance through strands of her blonde hair. He recognized the scene from an evening last fall when the Kingsleys and Brightons had gathered for a meal on the still-green lawns of Ravensleigh.

The lighting complemented her pale yellow dress and spread a heavenly glow about her. She looked like something from a vision, the light casting a softness about her face and figure that was dreamlike, except for the almond-shaped, sapphire eyes that were so sharp and clear he could see each individual eyelash that outlined them.

Crispin met the sapphires from across the table, the lids beneath them lifting ever so slightly. Audra could smile with her eyes as no one could, and she had a smile just for him. It had been a memorable moment for Crispin; the first time he saw in her features the change from girlhood to young woman. He marveled as a gentle breeze wrapped around her, and gold curls danced along a newly defined line that ran from ear to chin. Gone was the fuller-faced look of her younger self, and the changes were not limited to her face. As Audra lifted slender fingers to play with a sapphire pendant necklace that matched her eyes, a fuller bosom that had replaced her formerly flat chest was visible, and with each breath new, womanly curves rose and fell from the depths of her bodice. At that moment, Crispin thought his lovely Audra had come into an elegance he had not seen carved into the most masterful works of art.

He had loved her as a boy, and now he both loved and ached for her as a man. With his beloved yet across from him, the distance drew a hollow feeling to the pit of his stomach. If only she were nearer to him. If only she were beside him, that he could put his arm around her. If only he could whisper sweet nothings to her while breathing in the sweet-pea-scented perfume she so often dabbed behind her porcelain earlobes.

Another breeze, cool in the fall air, carried the delicate fragrance to his nostrils, warming him. A tingling sensation ran from the back of his neck down his spine, and he fidgeted in his chair. That she should be so near to him, that he should see her and smell her, and yet he could neither touch her nor have a private word with her was insufferable.

Audra herself had only contributed to his tormented condition. She had pulled him from the house before anyone had given a thought to going outside and allowed him the rare opportunity of kissing her. It was their most passionate kiss to date, and the sight of her afterwards, flushed and breathless, had not left him. In fact, the image was burned indelibly in his mind's eye, and he allowed his eyes to search her mouth now from across the table. He yearned for the pouty, pink lips that protruded from narrow corners—and that she caught him looking did not halt him from doing so. The blush in her cheeks only served to intensify his sudden and overwhelming longings, and he bit down on his teeth in frustration. Even should she allow him to kiss her again, kissing would no longer be enough.

Crispin rested his hand on the table and slid it toward her. He reached out for her own, slender hand, only to grasp into nothingness. The memory faded from his eyes, and he awoke to the darkness of his room. He rubbed his eyes before thrusting his forehead into the palms of his hands and rested his elbows in his lap.

Audra…Oh, Audra…

They intended to marry each other. They had discussed it many times, and he had never doubted her feelings. She was so affectionate toward him that it had never occurred to Crispin that she might fall in love with someone else if given the opportunity to meet other men. And he, for his part, had mentally and emotionally given himself over to her so completely that it seemed they were already one flesh.

Audra… He groaned and fell back into his pillow. *What are you doing?*

• • •

"Whatever do you mean, *stay in London*?" cried Audra.

Lady Sutherland did not trouble herself to lift her eyes from her embroidery. "Lady Audra, do you think we have traveled all this way to London to leave within the week? Oh, my dear, what an idea! We are to stay for several weeks, at least."

"Several weeks! Lady Sutherland," Audra appealed, "I appreciate you bringing me here. But I have been presented at court. I have danced at Almack's. I have no further purpose here. I am anxious to return to Thornton."

"For what?"

"For *what*?" repeated Audra, pacing the room. "To be married. *To your nephew.* Surely this is no surprise to you. I will write to Lady Brighton and have her send someone to pick me up."

"My dear, you must allow yourself the opportunity to explore all your options. I cannot support a decision you will certainly regret once you are married."

"With all due respect, Lady Sutherland, how can you know what I will or will not regret?"

The lady at last met Audra's gaze with a dumbfounded air. "Your outspokenness is highly unbecoming, Lady Audra. You should respect the knowledge of your elders. I only have your best interest at heart." She added, "Also, did it not occur to you that I may have reason to remain in London? I have friends and family in town whom I have not seen in some years. And I intend to visit with them."

"Why did you say nothing of this before we left?"

"I do not recall you mentioning your intention to leave London almost immediately upon your arrival."

At this, Audra paused. Had her intentions been so clear in her own mind that she had never actually discussed them with Lady Sutherland?

"You knew the reason I was coming," she said at last. Of that much, Audra was certain.

"Yes, to be introduced to society," returned the lady.

"So that my engagement to Lord Crispin might be made official."

Lady Sutherland sighed, as if exasperated by the tantrums of a two-year-old child. "Have you considered Lord Crispin may simply be interested in your inheritance?"

Audra's mouth fell, and she prayed quickly for restraint in her words. "*What?*"

"He is a second son, my dear. You are an heiress—to Kingsley Manor, no less, and do I understand there is an Irish estate, as well? Wyndgate, is it?"

"You would speak of your nephew in such a manner?" cried Audra in disbelief. "And even if all he cared about was my inheritance, would you not be glad for him? Would you not wish exactly such a circumstance for him?"

"I am partial toward my own sex, Lady Audra, family or otherwise. And whether or not you believe me, I am putting your interests above my nephew's."

"*I love him!*"

"Love can wait. Tonight, we have a ball to attend, and I fear you are in need of a nap."

Chapter Six

April 16, 1836—London

Over the course of a few weeks, Audra's emotions had danced in a wind of shock, anger, and depression. The shock of realizing Lady Sutherland was in no hurry to bring her home was the first of these emotions, and it did not disappear when the anger began to settle in. Now, still with no word from home, Audra had grown increasingly depressed, and her heart lay heavy in her chest.

Audra quickly became familiar with the amusements of London. Weeks passed—weeks of attending concerts and driving in the park, going to operas and parties until five in the morning, unwanted gentlemen calling on her—while she awaited word from Thornton. Audra walked in a daze among the vendors of the Pantheon Bazaar and the tightrope walkers of Vauxhall Gardens; she dined silently at the Star & Garter, avoiding conversation with Lady Sutherland at all costs. The woman went about her days as cheerful as ever, quite as if no unpleasant exchange had ever occurred between them. Meanwhile, with every appearance of the lady, Audra relived that dreadful conversation; how she had stormed upstairs and scribbled passionate letters home detailing the nature of the exchange. Yet none of her notes to her father, Lady Brighton, or Rhianna had been answered, and as the days passed, no one arrived to take her home.

Tired from pacing the wood planks of her room, Crispin's six-month-old baby portrait clutched tightly in her arms, Audra paused beside her windowsill to look out over the city of London. The scene sickened her, and she moved hastily to her bed. Falling back onto her blankets, she dropped the portrait beside her, stared up at the canopy, and envisioned home.

Crispin seemed so close to her, and as she recalled their private moments in the days before she left Thornton, she could almost feel him. She could feel his fingers wandering along her waist, playfully tugging the strings at the back of her dress. She could feel his warm lips brush lightly against the base of her neck. *I love you, Audra*, he confessed in a breathy whisper. *I love you.*

Her heart had fluttered wildly under his touch that day, just as it fluttered now, and she writhed under the memory. His hot breath prickling against her skin made her every extremity tingle, both then and now, and she was unwilling to let the daydream go. Her own breathing quickened, and Audra clutched at her waist as she lay on the bed, her corset suffocating and restrictive.

Crispin…

She bit her lower lip as she remembered his body against hers, the strength of his arms as he pulled her closer, and the fiery desire in his eyes when she refused him a kiss. She shivered at his groans, and the pit of her stomach nearly convulsed when he licked the ring from her necklace and into his mouth in frustration.

"When you have me," she said, curiosity overtaking her, "will you be sweet?"

He pulled back suddenly, with a look of shock in his eyes, and he stood over her, breathing heavily. "My God, Audra…"

His face contorted with a horrified look, and he pushed her farther away from him, arms extended, his hands cupping her shoulders.

"Well?" she demanded. She felt herself begin to shiver. "I don't want to find out *then*. I want to know *now*."

His mouth was open, but no words came out. She knew it had not been a ladylike question, but still…

"The truth is," she told him, her eyes falling, "I'm…afraid."

Crispin drew a breath, in relief she thought, but she couldn't tell for sure. He took her face in his hands and pulled her head to his lips. He pressed them against her forehead, and she closed her eyes tightly as he dug his fingers into her hair.

Then, shaking his head, he leaned back and looked at her earnestly. "I *love* you, Audra," he said again. "I love you, and when you are mine, I will *make love* to you." Crispin wrapped his arms around her and pulled her close, holding her tightly. "I'm sorry, Audra. I'm so sorry I frightened you." Crispin took her hands in his and held them to his breast. "There is nothing to fear," he promised.

She met his ice-blue eyes and melted inwardly. Then, turning her palms upward, he kissed her wrists gently, sending bolts of lightning through her. She gasped audibly at his touch, and her breast rose and fell with each brush of his lips.

"Kiss me," she said breathlessly.

At last, she invited him in, and Crispin threw her arms over his shoulders and leaned over her. His heavily fringed eyes met hers with a wanting expression, but he kept his wide lips inches from hers. Audra parted her lips and tightened her arms about his neck, but Crispin restrained himself.

"No," he told her at last.

"No?" she repeated, her brows furrowing.

He shook his head, a pained expression on his face, and he gulped. "Now, we wait."

Crispin released her from his grasp, with the exception of her one hand which he playfully nibbled.

Oh, why hadn't he kissed her? She had wanted him to so badly.

"I'll be waiting," she heard him say, and saw his smiling face as he urged her back to the house.

"Oh!" she cried aloud, and flung herself from the bed. Audra soon stood brooding over her writing desk, lifting the ring she kept tucked between her breasts by the chain and clutching it in a fist at her throat.

Should she write again? She glared down at the gold and ivory table where lay the most recent notes she had received from Secret Admirer. She scowled at them, if for no reason other than it was the only written correspondence she had received from anyone. Even last night, when the first of two more letters made its appearance under her glass of lemonade, and the second on her chair at dinner, she had been annoyed and refused to open them. In both instances, Audra stuffed them roughly into her reticule and wished the man behind them would just stop.

Snatching one irritably, she unfolded it. Treating it none too gently, she shook out its folds and read:

My Dear Lady Audra…

Her eyes began to fall to the first line, but reverted back sharply to the opening address.

"*My?*" she repeated aloud.

The verbalization of it only served to give further disturbance to the additional word.

My, indeed.

Audra took a deep, frustrated breath and continued:

My Dear Lady Audra,

I was pleased to see you found my note this evening. From your reaction, I sensed your understanding that its contents were for your eyes only. I wish to thank you for the respect you have shown me by keeping my secret, your secret. Know that there is one in attendance tonight who holds you in high regard.

Your Secret Admirer

As she read, she recalled stuffing the first of the notes into her reticule without reading it. He had watched her? Was he *always* watching? An uncomfortable feeling washed over her, and…

My God, she thought, as for the first time it suddenly occurred to Audra that the longer this dragged on, the more emotionally devoted Secret Admirer was likely to become. Oh, that she could have told him early on, before a second note ever was written! Now she had collected more letters than she cared to count, and they were turning more intimate. If only he had revealed himself weeks ago, she could have let him down gently, and he could have focused his efforts on other, *eligible* ladies.

There was a knock at the door, and her lady's maid, Molly, entered. "Lady Audra? It's time to dress you for the theater tonight."

Audra bid her enter, and she made her way to the closet. "Will it be the blue dress tonight, Lady Audra?"

The blue dress. The very words brought her back to the first days after Lady Sutherland voiced her intention to remain in London. Audra had been in a state of shock when the lady, who genuinely seemed to want Audra to enjoy her London stay, brought her to a dressmaker on Bond Street. She was fitted for several new outfits, and the sapphire dress was now in her possession. She wanted to hate it, but seeing how well it matched her eyes it was impossible to do so, and she accepted it was silly to take her situation out on the poor, lovely gown.

"Yes, Molly, thank you."

She admired it, sighing as the maid spread it out on the bed. Even in her pretty new dress, there was only one person she wished to wear it for, and *he* would not be at the theater to see it.

• • •

Audra followed Lady Sutherland through the Theater Royal, Covent Garden saloon toward their private box, forcing a smile at acquaintances along the way. She was glad for those who gave a simple acknowledgement from their seats as they spoke with other companions from the red velvet cushions of the stone benches lining the walls. Nothing of the tall statues or the pedestals upon which they sat could impress her. Even *Don Juan of Austria* would hold no interest for her tonight, as the predominately yellow, gold, and white colors of the main room reminded her of own bedchamber in the townhouse—and that she was yet residing in that room when she ought to be in Thornton.

The sight of Lord Everton outside their box did little to lift her spirits, even if he was one of only two people she had grown fond of seeing. Embeth, she suspected, would be along shortly, and Audra always kept a sharp eye out for her.

Lord Everton had become something of a fixture in their nightly activities, and today he greeted them as he always did— as if the arrival of their party of two was the only event of the evening.

Audra had fallen into a routine with him that seemed to suit the both of them very well: on each meeting, he would flirt with her, she would remind him of her engaged status, and from then on they behaved as old friends. He had a unique way of engaging her interest that she credited with keeping her sanity in her imprisoned state. Not only that, but he served willingly as a confidant when the occasion required it, and sympathized with her as she awaited letters from home.

Lady Sutherland stopped to speak with a female acquaintance, and Audra was glad when Lord Everton offered his arm to escort her to her seat.

"You are looking especially lovely tonight, Lady Audra," he complimented. "Your gentleman back home is a fortunate fellow to have claimed such a beauty. If I may be so bold, I have never been so jealous of a man I have never met."

"Oh, Lord Everton, how you go on," she said flippantly. "Pray, how are you doing in your search for a Lady Everton?"

She dared not tease him about the rumors of him meeting with the night's lead actress, whose performances, she heard, were not limited to the stage.

"Assuming you have not blinded me to them," he said, "I have met some charming girls these last few weeks. I expect my plan to leave London with a wife will see through to the finish."

She thought him more flirtatious than usual, but overall ignored his playful comments. Audra had no energy to concern herself with a few, teasing lines from one of the only persons in London who did not annoy or frustrate her.

"Well, I'm glad…"

Audra stopped suddenly, dropping his arm as they approached her seat in the box. There, resting on her cranberry cushion, lay a folded note addressed to "Lady Audra" in a familiar script.

"Oh, this has to stop!" she cried, reaching for it.

"What is it?" Lord Everton asked, alarm laced through his voice.

Forgetting Lord Everton's presence, Audra unfolded the note and read:

"My Dearest…"

"Oh!" she cried again at the inscription.

Now Secret Admirer had overstepped his bounds. The sight of "*My Dearest*" as a standalone greeting, not even followed by "Lady Audra," inclined her to toss the note off the ledge of their box. Indeed, she attempted to do so, before Lord Everton interceded.

"What is this?" he asked, gently taking hold of her wrist and examining the paper clenched in her hand.

She tightened her fingers around it so severely she crumpled the note into a wrinkled ball.

"It's nothing," she told him, pulling her arm from him.

"It's *something*," he replied, eyeing her with concern.

Audra huffed. "Fine. Here," she said, offering it to him. "Take it, if you want it. I certainly do not."

She allowed the note to fall from her fingers, and he caught it. His gaze met hers with a curious expression, then fell to the folded note.

"Lady Audra, I hardly feel I have the authority to read your private notes. Why do you not just tell me what is going on?"

"Lord Everton, I wish you would read it," she told him passionately. "Read it, and then tell me what to do, because something must be done, and I hardly know what."

He hesitated, watching her.

"Please," she added. "Read it before Lady Sutherland comes in."

Reluctantly, he nodded. "As you wish."

Audra crossed her arms and sat fuming in her cranberry seat. She marveled that it was the first time Secret Admirer had evoked such powerful emotions in her. Perhaps it was the frustration of her inability to escape London emitting from her every pore, but Audra suspected not. This man, whoever he was, had not given her any opportunity to deflect his advances, all while his own emotions were running away with him. No longer were these notes a curious pastime to be tossed carelessly aside. They were a heavy weight upon her shoulders, a responsibility thrust upon her, with a person's heart in the balance and no foreseeable release from the situation.

She glanced sideways at Lord Everton as he held the blasted thing, and waited silently for his response.

His eyes scanned it quickly, and then lifted back to her. "Am I to take it this is not the first note you have received from your 'Secret Admirer'?" Her silence confirmed his suspicion. "How long has this been going on?"

She shrugged. "Since I arrived. Only, I should say they are more frequent now. I received two almost together last night."

His eyes widened. "And in the weeks since you've arrived, has he not come forward?"

"No. I haven't a clue who he is. I have never been so annoyed!"

This evoked a disconcerted laugh from him, and he said, "This Secret Admirer likely has little idea that his love notes are resulting in your annoyance."

"Well, he should," she told him, sourly.

"He seems to me a clever sort of fellow. After all, aren't girls supposed to like love notes?"

Audra frowned viciously at him. "Not when you are engaged to someone else! Not when love notes are from strangers! And not when you have no way of telling them to stop!"

He nodded, as if this last provided him with a clearer understanding. His eyes grew both kind and serious, and any thought of teasing her on the subject that might have come to mind was never attempted.

"What does Lady Sutherland say of these letters?" he asked.

"I am speaking to Lady Sutherland as infrequently as possible," Audra said tartly. "Lord Everton, I really don't know how to resolve this. This man must be told to direct his attentions elsewhere. What should I do?"

Lord Everton pressed his lips together and held the note back out to her. "I'm afraid there is not much to be done until he reveals himself."

Audra shot him a glance as she heard the sound of nearing voices. Quickly, she stuffed the letter into her glove as Lady Sutherland entered the box.

• • •

Audra fidgeted in her seat during the first act of *Don Juan of Austria*, Secret Admirer's note scratching at her wrist. She was ever conscious of it as an incessant itch she dared not scratch. And whereas she had had no interest earlier in knowing its full contents, she now began to wonder what words had been laid before

Lord Everton's eyes. She allowed her mind to wander so freely she had not a clue what was taking place on the stage below her.

At intermission, Audra left Lady Sutherland for the privacy of the powder room. There were other girls scattered about, but none she knew. Satisfied they would not trouble her; she pulled the note from her glove, unfolded it with quivering hands, and read:

> My Dearest,
> I flatter myself that you were hoping I would reappear tonight. As if I could keep away! Ardent feelings grow for you daily, and I must say there is not one who could match your loveliness in all of London. Your fair features keep me in a fair state of hypnosis. Your blonde locks have fastened themselves around my heart. Give me a sign that you wish to know my identity, and I may be willing to grant a hint.
> Your Secret Admirer

She lifted her eyes enough to search the powder room through her lashes, as something of a tightness pulled across her chest. Of course, there were no men *here*, but she was relieved nonetheless to find it confirmed. It was not very much her way to feel fear, though she had not experienced many situations that should rouse the emotion. However, with this note, she was distinctly aware of the discomforting feeling of being watched, and for the first time, its author seemed more of a prowler than a secret admirer.

"There you are!" Audra turned to the sound of Embeth's voice. "Lord Everton told me I would find you in here. Is the play not wonderful—oh, dear, what is wrong?"

Audra held the note up to her, and Embeth recognized its style right away. Embeth was the only other person Audra had discussed the notes with, and she had read the recent ones.

Embeth took the letter and examined its contents. "They are more frequent now," she said upon finishing. "This one is quite poetic…"

"I want him to stop," Audra told her, pacing the floor.

Embeth redirected her comments. "He always says he is in the audience, or he will be in attendance," Embeth noted. "Have you ever noticed anyone who…?"

"Never." Audra waved her hand-painted, French *brisé* fan wildly as a wave of anger washed over her. "And I have looked, believe me."

Embeth led her to a pink embroidered settee. "Sit a moment, won't you?"

Audra allowed her friend to pull her down beside her.

"Follow my thoughts, Audra, please. Before you get yourself too worked up," she said, gently taking Audra's fan before her clenched fingers could snap its blond horn sticks in two, "there is the possibility…"

"Don't," Audra said, knowing where the thoughts of Embeth's fanciful side would lead her. "I am not interested in this man."

"What if he is wonderful?" asked Embeth with a smile. "What if he is as charming and sincere as these letters make him out to be? It could be viewed as romantic."

"I am committed to Crispin," Audra said. "The man who is writing these letters is allowing his feelings to run away with him. He must be told he has no chance of a relationship with me, and he makes it impossible to do so. By his refusal to approach me as any normal man would, I am beginning to think him a coward."

Embeth took the hint that Audra would hear nothing in the realm of praise. "This Crispin of yours must be someone very special to elicit such a powerful commitment," she told her.

"He is the love of my life, Embeth. A handful of love letters from a secret admirer are not going to change that. And they're ridiculous!" she cried. "'Ardent feelings grow for you daily'? What does he know of me beyond my 'blonde locks'? He is nonsensical."

"Well, he seemed to be opening up the opportunity for you to discover his identity."

"Oh, yes, 'a sign' will get me 'a hint'! I am not going to encourage him by playing along, Embeth."

She patted Audra's hand. "I wish I could help in some way."

Audra drew as deep a sigh as her restrictive clothing would allow. "Your listening ear has been a great comfort, Embeth, and I fear I have abused it terribly. I'm sorry for being so ill-humored."

"No apologies, please. I know how distressed you are."

"I'm sure he's harmless, of course. I just…I don't want to be the cause of a broken heart."

Embeth handed the note back to Audra. "I do wonder," she said, watching as Audra stuffed it back into her glove, "why he does this."

"There is only one explanation, Embeth," Audra declared confidently. "He must have terrible warts. He must make his lady fall in love with him before ever they meet."

The girls gave way to a spurt of laughter, and Audra was glad to find some of the tension was released.

"Let us change the subject. Have you had much opportunity to spend time with Lord Wesley this evening?"

Embeth blushed. "Not nearly enough for my liking, but I daresay half the evening."

"Well," cried Audra, "considering the evening is only half over, I see he is making the most of it!"

Secretly, Audra wished every day that Embeth would fall for Lord Everton. She liked them both so well, she was sure they would be excellent together. But dear Embeth was wild about Lord Wesley, and Lord Everton never mentioned Embeth—or any other female—as an interest of his.

Ah, but she could hope.

•••

After the play concluded, Embeth and her mother met Audra and Lady Sutherland in their box. The former were heading to Lord Meryton's home on Park Lane, and wanted to be sure the latter were doing the same.

"Audra," Embeth whispered, "who is that man that keeps staring at you?"

"A man?" asked Audra, stilling her fan. "Where?"

She turned to the direction Embeth had been looking, across the horseshoe auditorium to a box on the second tier.

"He's…well, he was…Oh, dear, he's gone," Embeth said, searching along the balcony rail.

"Can you describe him?"

"Middle-aged, not very heavy, nor very thin," she began. "Do you think it could be *him*?"

"Perhaps! Have you ever seen him before?"

"No, I don't think so," Embeth told her. "If it *is* him," she added, "and since he seems to be everywhere, perhaps he will follow you to the Merytons."

"Well, then," said Audra, preparing her mind for bravery, "you must help me, Embeth. Tonight, I hope to find him, and put an end to his nonsense!"

Chapter Seven

It was a long, quiet carriage ride with Lady Sutherland. The lady, seeming always exhausted from her never-ending chatting amongst friends, was frequently, blessedly quiet around Audra, and as Audra had decided it best weeks ago not to speak with her companion unless absolutely necessary, she found this lack of communication quite satisfactory. There was, however, one question Audra knew she should like to ask her patroness, and when they drew close to the Meryton's, she addressed her.

"Do you not think it odd that there has been no correspondence from Thornton?"

"No, not at all," she replied, fanning herself and looking disinterestedly out the window. She responded as if they had been speaking all along.

"I wrote my first letters to the Ladies Brighton weeks ago," Audra pointed out. "And to my father."

Audra braced herself for a sermon on how her family likely agreed she should not rush her Season to end, but the lady did not take that road.

"They are no doubt very involved with the baby," she said. "I would not over think it. As you know, I also wrote to them of our safe arrival, and have received no response."

Audra was sure anyone else would have thought it odd, but the lady's response was undisturbed, utterly without suspicion. She considered briefly that Lady Sutherland's responses to anything other than the absolute present were always short and always disinterested. Indeed, if the subject was not of Almack's, London, the theater, or their current circle of friends, any attempt at conversation with Lady Sutherland came to a rapid standstill.

She quickly gave up the exchange, and Audra was never so glad for the carriage to come to a halt. Lady Sutherland's company was becoming less and less tolerable, and her refusal to speak on subjects other than those *she* wished to discuss was, in Audra's mind, selfish, and she had little forbearance for people who thought only of themselves.

It was not the first time Audra had met Lord Meryton. He was a long-time acquaintance of her father's and had visited Kingsley Manor many times over the years. Only his detached, London house on Park Lane was new to her. Known as Ashford House, the elegant Palladian mansion, whose architect broke its traditional symmetry with some Gothick forms, stood on its own parkland overlooking Hyde Park. Some of its fashionable features were the rusticated stonework on the ground floor of the otherwise stucco building, and a preference for numerous Venetian windows.

They entered the large front doorway with engaged columns to find a great many Palladian details within. The hall was masculine, filled with lions and griffins, but Audra found beauty in its Ionic columns. A much more feminine interior filled the rest of the house, and there was no want of cherubs and flowers and nude ladies in the fireplace surrounds.

After greeting Lord and Lady Meryton, they entered the ballroom, and Audra caught sight of Embeth DeBlock. She swiftly made her way to her, leaving Lady Sutherland to her own choice of companions.

"Oh! Audra, you will never guess." Embeth looked about her discreetly, and with an elegance that awed Audra. "I have found our man from the theater, just as we hoped."

"Have you, indeed?"

"Yes, let us make our way to the balcony. Perhaps I can point him out to you from there."

Audra followed her up the stairs to a far corner of the balcony, and the two girls leaned eagerly against the edge of polished, dark wood railing. "I was closer to him this time. He is an ugly sort of fellow, Audra. He has a warped, crooked nose and terribly bucked teeth. He was looking around him, as for something lost. Searching for you, I imagine."

"Well, as we suspected," Audra said, "assuming he *is* Secret Admirer, his only hope for love is to make his lady fall in love with him before she can lay eyes on him."

At this moment, Lord Everton sauntered over. He was looking very fashionable in his modern, square-toed boots, white tuxedo shirt, and silk vest, and Audra secretly hoped Embeth would take notice.

He seemed to be enjoying himself. "What are you girls giggling over?"

Audra threw her arms behind her back and rocked on the balls of her feet. "Oh, not you, Lord Everton, never fear. What brings you to this corner of the room?"

"The company, of course." Glancing briefly about them, he added, "It seems from this position, your chance of avoiding dancing for the majority of the evening is quite good, Lady Audra."

"I hope to be very successful, thank you. Though I fear I am unfairly keeping Miss DeBlock from the floor."

"Not at all," she assured.

Lord Everton extended his hand to Embeth, and she blushed deeply. "Would you allow me the honor?"

She threw a glance at Audra, and she encouraged her to accept. "Counting down the minutes until the evening ends need not be a group venture. Go with Lord Everton. I insist."

Embeth accepted his hand, and Audra smiled to herself as they left, laughing at her matchmaking ways. Not that Lord Wesley wasn't agreeable; he just wasn't as agreeable to Audra as Lord Everton, and certainly not as good looking. They would make such a fine couple, she thought, and should they end up together, Audra was prepared to give herself full credit for the match.

Growing tired and irritable, Audra was not sorry to see them go. She didn't mind watching them from her quiet corner. Resting her hands on the railing, she watched the floor below where Embeth and Lord Everton made their way into the midst of the thickening crowd and a lively orchestra followed the conductor into a quadrille.

Audra yawned and wished her corset would allow her to take a deeper breath. She was suddenly conscious of just how exhausted she was, and she pushed herself away from the railing. To her left, a floral-fabric, ivory-painted chair beckoned her, and she took a few steps toward it.

Just then, she felt her face drain of its color at the sight of another folded piece of paper with the familiar splotched handwriting on the floor beneath the chair. And not only that, but a burr maple jewelry box with brass lion's paws lay as a paperweight.

She looked around her but saw no one in her immediate vicinity. Thoughts raced through her mind so rapidly she could hardly make them out—until she settled on one:

Leave it.

She felt suddenly brilliant. Why should she take it? Yes, she knew it was from *him*, and yes, she knew it was for *her*. But what better way to tell Secret Admirer she was not interested than to ignore his letter—and now a gift, as well? Curiosity was the only thing that could have prompted her to take it, and Audra was determined to out-smart curiosity.

How is that for a sign? she thought.

With her cozy corner quiet no more, she turned with renewed energy in the direction opposite, down the grand staircase, and made way for the crowds that lined the polished dance floor below.

• • •

A gallopade began when Audra accepted a dance from a kindly gentleman whom she recalled being introduced to, but whose name escaped her. She found it not at all awkward that she had forgotten his name, as there was no instance in their conversation in which, "Oh my, you didn't!" or "What a story you tell!" did not substitute.

Often, she found herself beside Lord Everton and Embeth, and she was pleased to see them smiling widely together. Lord Everton occasionally made silly faces at Audra, and she suppressed a giggle so as to avoid explaining the relationship to Lord Whatever-His-Name-Was.

As the song neared its end, Lord Everton met Audra's gaze with his most ridiculous of glances, and in so doing lost his footing on the floor. He released Embeth just as he collided with Audra's nameless partner, and she herself went flying into the arms of a man standing at the edge of the floor.

"Oh! I'm so terribly sorry!" she cried to him, as the boys on the dance floor clambered to their feet. "My goodness, thank you for catch—"

Audra met the man's peering gaze and was silenced. His gray eyes looked at her so intensely, and without blinking, that she lost her sentence mid-way. Indeed, he seemed very disagreeable, and did not smile, and she got the instant sensation that he was enraged with her.

Dropping her eyes to collect her thoughts, she looked back to him only when she knew how to proceed.

"I thank you for catching me, sir. It was quite an accident, I assure you."

With her footing secure, she released her hands from his dress coat sleeves and went to smooth her skirts, but the stranger tightened his grip around her forearms.

Hesitantly, she told him, "I am balanced, I believe. It is quite safe to release me."

For a moment, Audra felt sure he had no intention of doing so. Thankfully, Lord Everton and her nameless partner were soon at her side, and the stranger dropped his hands, saying nothing.

Commotion at once swarmed her, and Audra was left to promise the boys she was unharmed. In fact, they fought for her attention with such distraction, that when Audra looked back, the stranger was gone.

Embeth was soon at her side, "Audra, are you alright?"

"Did you see that man?" she asked. "The one with gray eyes and salt-and-pepper hair? The one who caught me?"

"I saw nothing but commotion," Embeth told her. "Are you hurt?"

And Audra, with a profusion of promises that she was quite all right, soon began to question her own assurances. The stranger's reaction had disturbed her tremendously, and she hoped not to see him again.

•••

And yet she did see him again—and she saw him seeing her. Watching her. Glaring at her. Everywhere she looked, his face would appear. At the stairs. Near the orchestra. On the balcony. This man whom she had never before seen was suddenly ubiquitous. And it came as no surprise to Audra that no one troubled to speak with him. Every stance, every line of his face was unapproachable.

A few hours into the evening, one such encounter left Audra uncomfortably close to the stranger, and she met Lord Everton's glance from across the room. The look on her face must have frightened him, for his reaction was swift. In almost a single bound, he was beside her, urging from her an explanation for the anxious expression in her eyes.

"There is a gentleman I would swear is watching me."

"Is that all?" Dismissing her concerns with a laugh, Lord Everton asked, "Have not we all done the same?"

"There is a distinct difference between looking at a woman and prowling after her. I have caught him on several occasions and admit that I am now quite uncomfortable." Audra waved her fan anxiously through the warm, damp air. "It is the same gentleman who assisted me during our little tumble, and he looks very sour."

With her last words, she rushed her fan to her mouth with a gasp. Secret Admirer's note and gift flashed through her mind, and without any explanation to Lord Everton she made her way up the grand staircase and along the balcony to the chair where she had left both. Lord Everton fell quickly into step with her swift pace, graciously holding his questions until she reached her destination.

The note and the jewelry box were gone, and questions danced in Audra's mind: Was it him? Was he angry? What was Embeth's description of the man from the theater?

"What is it?" Lord Everton ventured, as she dropped onto the chair and looked at him.

"There was a letter. And a gift. And I left it."

Lord Everton seemed perplexed, but then his expression changed as she suspected he made the connection between the stranger that pursued her and Secret Admirer.

"You think it's him?" he asked. She nodded. "Can you point him out to me?"

"Of course, he is not here *now*," Audra told him. "Why should he be, at the moment of discovery?"

Suddenly, he chuckled. "Have you only come out in Society a few weeks ago and already come to have a prowler, Lady Audra?"

"Lord Everton, you mock me! Are you saying I have made the whole of this up?"

"Perhaps I think you want me to be jealous."

"You know very well I would not tease you so. Jealous, indeed! I want no such thing. It would disastrously end our relationship, and I need you desperately. You are almost my only friend in the whole of London."

"Very well, my lady, let us find this prowler. I shall threaten him at once."

• • •

It was a fruitless endeavor. Lord Everton and Audra made the rounds of the room and balcony for more than half an hour, and the prowler was nowhere to be found. Restlessly, Audra stood by while Lord Everton on several occasions became entangled in conversation with other guests. His popularity made her itch, and as another acquaintance stopped him, Audra caught sight of the prowler as he slipped through a door leading toward some of the Merytons' private back rooms.

Audra politely excused herself with a discreet signal to Lord Everton indicating the direction of her target. He offered a subtle nod as acknowledgement, though he looked very uneasy as she stole away bravely on her own.

Fearlessly, she opened doors to private rooms she knew she had no business peeking into. Surely, she thought, he must be in one of them, for he was not in the public rooms. Fortunately, her conscience was mostly silent on the matter of snooping around Lord Meryton's private quarters. And each time Audra opened a new door, she grew bolder and her conscience spoke even less to her.

The farther she traveled down this particular corridor, the farther she grew from the crowds. Indeed, everyone seemed to be enjoying themselves in the ballroom, the tearooms, and the gambling rooms. Here, there was no one, save for one door, from which even to innocent ears sounded the unmistakable moans and grunts of a man and woman in the throes of passion. Audra skipped that door, safely assuming neither of those persons was the prowler, as she was utterly convinced no woman would willingly subject herself to a man of such varied offenses of character. Not, at least, in the company present at Lord Meryton's.

Near the end of the hall, her search came to a sudden halt when she found herself standing not five feet from the dreaded prowler. He appeared from around the corner and stood motionless, staring.

And in his hand, he held a letter.

So he is Secret Admirer, she thought to herself.

Audra had hoped to speak to him, perhaps to reason with him, but the sight of him so frightened her that she stood immobilized, speechless, and afraid even to look behind to see if anyone was nearby if she called for help.

He spoke, instead, with a muffled, disgruntled voice. "You did not take my letter. Or my gift."

Audra slowly shook her head. He had a wild look in his eye, and Audra was certain he was not thinking with a sound mind. She feared any quick movements might cause him to do something rash, and she froze in position.

"Did you not like my letters?"

Audra mustered courage and spoke in a calm but clear voice. "I am engaged, sir. I wish I could have told you sooner."

He snickered. Audra stilled her breath.

"Engagement is no barrier to love," he said gruffly.

To love? she cried inwardly.

"You misunderstand my situation, sir..."

He held up his hand. "I do not, and I'll thank you not to mention it again." He held up the note in his hand. "I recommend you take this one. And I'll find you again before the night is out." He threw it to the ground at her feet, adding, "Do not attempt to fight this, my dear. There is only one outcome for us."

Before Audra could say another word, he stole away in the direction he had come.

Distressed, Audra dropped her shoulder against the wall and eyed the note on the ground. Whatever was she to do? Before this night, Secret Admirer had been just a lovesick bachelor with a taste for the theatrical. In her mind, she had envisioned him young, or at least younger, and certainly *sane*, someone with whom she could speak, who would comprehend her situation and, without taking offense, willingly continue his search for a wife with another well-bred, available lady. But *this*…

Audra scooped up the letter from the floor and entered the first door to her right, making sure to lock the handle behind her. She cared little what the room was, or who it was for, and noted only briefly a few scattered chairs and tall windows with long, blue curtains. That it was empty of people was all that mattered to her, and she leaned her back against the door and unfolded the note.

> My Pet,
>
> I will choose to defend your recent action of rejecting my note and gift by lifting you to the highest example of womanly modesty. I do admit awareness that propriety demands a respectable woman never accept a gift of jewelry from a man other than her husband. So I will retain my gift until such time arrives when it would be correct and appropriate for you to accept it.
>
> In the meantime, I have a special evening prepared for you tonight, my love. I shall not spoil the surprise here, but may the knowledge of my closeness to you this evening warm your heart, knowing, too, that our consummated love will soon come to fruition.
>
> Yours, S.A.

A knock at the door jolted through her spine. With a startled gasp, Audra jumped away from it, her heart knocking against her breast in reply. Pressing her hands against her bosom, the fear she had not been fully conscious of was now fully magnified.

"Lady Audra?"

The voice was Lord Everton's. "Oh!" she cried with relief. Instinctively, she moved to unlock the door. "Thank goodness it's you."

He approached her. "What are you doing here? Are you all right?"

"I…" She fell onto a sofa and examined the cabinet on the far wall. "I could use a glass of wine."

He followed her gaze, and with two long strides was beside the cabinet, examining its contents. Finding only a few bottles of port, he held one up to her.

"That will do," she said.

He poured her a glass at once. "You are out of breath," he noted, sitting beside her.

"Yes, well," she said, taking the port handed to her and taking a sip, "I suppose that is very observant, Lord Everton."

She allowed a larger sip to roll around on her tongue. Then she finished the glass. "Thank you," she coughed, placing the glassware on an end table.

"This is," he told her, "a sort of gentleman's room, you know."

"Are you saying I cannot pass for a gentleman?" she asked.

He smiled widely. "You most certainly could not."

She saw him look her over with a familiar gape. "Oh, stop it. There are plenty of girls at this ball for you to look at with that gaze."

He raised an eyebrow. "There may be many girls present, but cannot say I wish to look much at them."

"Good heavens! You are the one who said any lady would do."

He shrugged. "So I did. It seems you think people incapable of changing their minds."

"Change it all you like," Audra said, "but do not waste your efforts on me. I am an engaged woman, lest you forget."

"I have not forgotten that you are not *officially* engaged."

Audra tossed her head to the side in exasperation. "You cannot say I did not warn you."

"I consider myself properly and thoroughly warned," he said. "Now, what are you going to tell me about how you came to be in this room?"

Audra produced the note, and he read it over quickly.

"A special evening," he read, mockery in his voice. "*Consummated* love," he emphasized with a smile. He arched a humorous eyebrow. "He is quite a catch."

"I *saw* him," she told him. "I *spoke* with him." This silenced Lord Everton, and he waited patiently for her to elaborate. "Secret Admirer and the prowler are, indeed, one and the same. Worse, he could not be reasoned with. He said there was no obstacle to our love," she added, with revulsion.

Lord Everton rubbed his chin thoughtfully. "Since I last asked, have you spoken to Lady Sutherland about him?"

"Lord, no! I refuse to speak whole sentences to her until she returns me to Thornton. She gets nothing but 'yes' and 'no' from me at the moment."

Lord Everton tapped his fingers on his leg. "Lady Audra, would you be very against remaining close to me for the remainder of this evening? Perhaps you will have opportunity yet to point him out to me, if you can avoid sneaking around in the Merytons' private quarters."

Audra sighed and glanced at the room around her. "You mean I cannot stay here?"

A brief laugh escaped his lips. "No, I'm afraid that is not an option."

"Oh, very well." Her hands fell into her lap. "Thank you, I suppose."

He assisted her to her feet. "Not at all. Thank *you*."

"For what?"

"For significantly improving my evening."

"You are shameless!"

"Perhaps."

"Well, you will never be able to say I gave you any encouragement. Do not allow your heart to be broken, Lord Everton. I am already in the process of breaking another."

A tilt of his head acknowledged her statement, and he led her to the door with a crooked smile.

• • •

Lord Garrington was still adjusting his cravat after a rendezvous with his mistress when he caught sight of a familiar face in the hallway. He looked not once, not twice, but a third time, and despite the overindulgence of port that warmed his blood and swayed his balance, there was no question about the matter. His conclusion with each examination was the same—the man standing before him was not only known to him, but he was utterly, unquestionably without invitation to Lord Meryton's.

"You there!" Lord Garrington said, with admittedly slurred speech. "What is your business here?"

The man with salt-and-pepper hair glared at him in silence for a moment before turning his back on Lord Garrington.

"Where are you going?" asked the lord. When his second question also went unanswered, and the man was departing down the hall, he called, "Mr. Thackeray!"

The man stopped. Slowly, he turned.

Lord Garrington continued, "I am sure Lord Meryton will be very interested to know you are wandering through his private halls."

An awkward and silent standoff presided over the moment before the man named Thackeray returned. "Am I to understand that Lord Meryton approves of your own presence in his private quarters?"

The lord cared not to explain either the nature of his business there or his private arrangements with Lord Meryton. "I do believe it is *your* presence that will be of interest to him, and I must admit I look forward to having that conversation with him. So, if you will excuse me."

With that, Lord Garrington pivoted toward the direction of the ballroom. The last thing he heard was the charging of footsteps and the creaking of the wooden floor before he turned around and felt the shock of the man's fist pressed against his stomach. A dull throbbing set in, and the throbbing grew in intensity. Lord Garrington felt the warm sensation of fluid trickling down his belly. He looked down, and a wave of panic overtook him as he discovered the handle of a knife protruding from his gut. Then a sense of shock settled in as his body began to tremble.

Lord Garrington dropped to his knees. Simultaneously, Mr. Thackeray squatted down beside him.

"I am afraid," said Mr. Thackeray, his hoarse voice dark and sinister, "you will not be in a position to have that conversation with Lord Meryton."

Unable to respond, the lord collapsed backwards to the floor. Lord Garrington was detached from the sensation of Thackeray's hands around his ankles and the motion of being dragged down the hallway. He was acutely aware only of the sudden and ever-increasing pain that seized him before his vision went dark.

• • •

When Audra and Lord Everton returned to the ballroom, the music had stopped, and guests were wandering around in seemingly aimless circles. A few of the young ladies looked very alarmed, the young men very serious, and the rest of the assembly stood around stifling giggles.

"What is all the commotion?" Lord Everton asked a nearby acquaintance.

The tall gentleman let out a chuckle. "Lady Meryton's pug is on the loose. She has found her way under several of the ladies' skirts, and disappeared. Some of the men have taken wild leaps to catch her, but it seems the creature is quite determined to enjoy her newfound freedom a while longer. Dancing is altogether halted until she is captured, for fear she may be trampled on."

Audra looked over the rail to the floor below, and Lord Everton leaned beside her. The crowds were scattered, some ladies huddling together as if a great monster were loose amongst them. Their admirers walked about, wiping the sweat from their brows, each searching earnestly for the pug, no doubt hoping to be the hero of the evening.

"Let us join in the search for her, shall we?" asked Audra, thinking it just the remedy she needed to ease the effects of her stressful night.

She did not wait for Lord Everton's answer, but made her way through thick crowds for the stairs, delighted with the distraction. As she descended a few steps, it was as if she did not have a care in the world.

It was a blissful moment, not meant to last. A note was forced into her hand. Audra turned as the gentleman who put it there ascended the stairs and was quickly hidden by the throngs of people descending them.

"Wait!" she cried.

She turned to chase him, only the crowds would not allow it. She did not have the stature to fight them. Audra was whisked down the steps against her will, partly furious, partly terrified, to the landing at the center of the staircase.

She crumpled the note in her hand as Lord Everton shouldered past the masses and caught up to her. His wider berth and added height provided a shield to the crowds that would otherwise have forced her to the base of the stairs.

"You are a swift one, Lady Audra. How am I to…What is that look?"

"He was just here," Audra breathed. "It was him!"

"Are you sure?"

She held up the note, and he did not wait for further confirmation. Lord Everton twisted his neck back to look, and the rest of his body followed. With a bounding leap, he raced back up the stairs, pushing old and young aside to take three steps at a time in Secret Admirer's direction.

Audra picked up her skirts and followed after him, offering apologies and begging pardons along the way. She thought if Lord Everton could just reach the balcony, he could catch up to him. Secret Admirer had at least twenty years on Lord Everton, and there was nothing about his physique that would support swiftness.

Breathless and a bit faint, Audra stepped foot on the balcony and caught sight of Lord Everton's tailcoat as he disappeared through a familiar door to the left. The balcony was less crowded than the staircase, and it was easier to move through the bodies of guests, save for the disapproving stares and the gruff comments of older men and women to "slow down" and "do not run." Audra apologized the entire way, until she reached the door to the same hallway where she had earlier met Secret Admirer.

Neither Secret Admirer nor Lord Everton was in sight, and with her skirts rustling about her, she hurried down the hall, listening at the doors for movements or voices—any sign they might have entered one of the rooms.

"Stop there!" she heard Lord Everton cry.

Audra followed the sound of his voice to a room midway down the hall. The door was slightly ajar, and she swung it fully open with her hand before entering. Seeing Lord Everton leaning full-bodied over the balcony railing of an open window urged her forward.

"You'll fall and be killed!" Lord Everton shouted.

Audra met him at his side and looked over the railing. There, Secret Admirer was attempting to climb down the thick vines on the side of the building. He struggled to master the three stories down to the greensward below.

"Oh, please!"

Fearing for his life, Audra covered her mouth with her hands, and the note she had held fluttered to the grass below.

The sound of her voice stopped him midway, and he looked up. "I shall have you yet, my beloved!"

These words threw Lord Everton into a state, and he threw one leg over the railing. Before Audra could cry "*No!*" he was on his way down.

"You will not torment Lady Audra any further!" Lord Everton cried.

He moved so quickly down the side of the building, Audra was sure the vines would give way under the weight of both men, and she turned away, unable to look.

When at last she turned back, her fingers clawing into her bodice with fright, she watched as Lord Everton chased Secret Admirer along a grand avenue within the park until their figures disappeared into the darkness.

And then, with a loud *pop*, she heard a gunshot.

• • •

Audra knew not how long she stood peering from the balcony into the shadowy darkness that hid Lord Everton's fate, her throat tight and her stomach inclined to vomit. She knew only that when she returned to the ballroom, Lady Meryton's pug must have been found, for the scene of previous commotion had now returned to normal. And with a single glance at the faces around her, she knew the sound of the shot must have been unheard by the guests, as they all continued about their affairs without any cause for concern. The old men gambled, the old women gossiped, and the couples on the floor skipped merrily. The orchestra and the voices of the crowds must have drowned out the gunfire.

Audra was utterly alone in her panic. Fear for Lord Everton's safety washed over her, and she leaned against a nearby wall, rendered almost incapable of thought. Should she alert anyone to the events she had just witnessed? She lamented her young age and lack of experience and prayed for Solomonic knowledge.

A desperate glance around the room offered a glimpse of Embeth, twirling in the arms of Lord Wesley, her face flushed to the color of a tomato. She did not expect Embeth to have a solution anymore than she did, but at least she would have been someone with whom Audra could share her frightening tale. In a short while, she wished desperately she could pull her away from Lord Wesley.

Suddenly, the unpleasant voice of her patroness called out to her, and Audra exhaled audibly as she turned to her.

"Lady Audra, where have you been all evening? I have seen neither hide nor hair of you," said Lady Sutherland. "You are white as a ghost," she noted.

"Did you not see me with Lord Everton?" she asked, sickly. Audra's stomach twisted and she gripped her midriff. This was no time for a conversation with Lady Sutherland. She must get to the main doors and wait for Lord Everton's return.

If he returned.

"No," the lady replied. "I did not. Pray, where has Lord Everton gone to now?"

It suddenly occurred to her that she must tell Lady Sutherland. As much as she disliked and resented her, she would know what to do. She must tell her, Audra told herself over and over, in rapid succession. For Lord Everton, she *must*.

"Lady Sutherland, we must speak on a very serious subject."

Lady Sutherland was easily startled, and she looked at once as if a mouse had scurried across her foot. "Gracious me, you have my attention, Lady Audra."

Audra drew a breath. "Lady Sutherland, there is a man that has been pursuing me."

"A man?" She paused. "Who is this man?"

Audra hesitated. "I do not know who he is. Only that he has been pursuing me every night since my arrival in London."

"My dear," said Lady Sutherland, clasping her hands together, "you have recently come out in society. You are pretty. You are wealthy. Did you believe you could appear invisible, or avoid gentlemen seeking you out?"

Audra held her ground. "*This* man makes me very uncomfortable."

"Why?"

There is no going back now, she thought.

"Love letters," she said swiftly. "He coins himself my Secret Admirer."

"Oh, my dear," said Lady Sutherland with a romantic twinkle in her eyes. "I daresay he sounds quite likeable to me."

Audra's eyebrows rose. "I have no interest in receiving such letters! Not only that, but I fear he has become quite obsessed, and I had an opportunity to tell him of my disinterest, but as it happens, he is quite deranged! Please understand me. I am quite literally afraid."

"Why have you not said anything of this man before?" Lady Sutherland asked.

It was a fair question. She had a fair answer.

"Lord Everton did not chase after him in my defense before tonight, and now he has climbed out the window of the upper floor and, Lady Sutherland, I heard a gunshot!"

The lady leapt where she stood. "Good heavens, child!"

"I am so afraid for Lord Everton's safety. I don't know what to do! What *should* we do?"

Lord Everton himself answered the question. "Dare I hope you would have missed me had I perished?"

Audra clutched her chest at the sound of his voice, and, turning to him, it took all her power not to throw her arms around him.

"Your prowler is gone, for now," he told her, as she remained speechless.

"I heard a gunshot," Audra managed. "You are not hurt?"

"Hurt! Ha! I shot at him," he told her proudly. "He avoided me, though. Spry old fellow, though you wouldn't think it. But not to worry, Lady Audra. I daresay I scared him off for now. I'd be surprised if we see him again anytime soon."

"Oh! Lord Everton, I...I hardly know what to say. Did you recognize him? Was he at all familiar to you?"

"Regrettably, no," he said. "I will say, he has quite a mind thinking an ugly sort of fellow like him could ever win a prize such as yourself."

"You are quite a brave man, Lord Everton," Lady Sutherland injected, recovering quickly and visibly enamored with Lord Everton. "Yes, indeed, you are very brave to go hunting down prowlers for vulnerable young ladies." She shot a sideways glance at Audra as she added, "Any young debutante would be fortunate to have you around."

Audra agreed audibly, echoing Lady Sutherland's sentiments. She praised him highly, perhaps too highly to be entirely appropriate, but her emotions had been so thoroughly abused throughout the evening, she only knew that Lord Everton was a hero—and despite the dangers he willingly encountered for her sake, he was safe.

"Well, this is quite outrageous," Lady Sutherland said, fanning herself. "I'm afraid the whole affair has made me feel quite weak in the knees. Excuse me while I take a seat." She retreated to a blue settee against the far wall, allowing them a more intimate moment to recuperate from the events of Secret Admirer.

Overtaken by happiness and relief, Audra thanked Lord Everton even more passionately without the hovering ears of Lady Sutherland. She hardly heard the words with which she expressed herself, so focused was she on the *how*, and her greatest concern was that her thanks be of the most genuine, heartfelt sort. She noted with a distant awareness that the words flowed more effortlessly now that Lady Sutherland had withdrew from them, and in the multitude of sentences he did not interrupt her.

When at last she was in fear of repeating herself, she left him with a beaming smile, and he met it with one of his own.

"Lady Audra, would you dance with me?" he asked.

She took his arm, and they began to make their way to the floor. Audra looked up at him, grateful to have found such a friend. She noted the look in his face was tender, even adoring, but she allowed these expressions and did not offer any words of discouragement. She hadn't the energy to scold him when all she wanted was to enjoy his safe return, assuring herself that he certainly would have done the same for any lady in such a circumstance.

Hand-in-hand, they assumed their positions for a country dance when a woman Audra did not know came crying hysterically down the stairs. Everyone turned to examine the lady who paused at the landing, her hand upon her stomach and her body doubled over as if she was in pain.

She opened her mouth as if to speak, but appeared unable. She gasped for breath instead, her face swollen and damp from the tears that streamed unceasingly from her eyes. Several times, it seemed, she attempted to speak while the entire audience stared at her, dumbfounded. With her free hand, she clutched an object, which to Audra's horror appeared to be a very familiar burr maple jewelry box with brass lion's paws.

Lord Meryton was soon making his way through the crowds, when at last the lady gathered enough strength to communicate. With one word, she gave the sum of her misery:

"Murder!"

• • •

It was hours from the time of the collective gasp that had sounded over the crowd to when Audra and Lady Sutherland were permitted to return to Queen Anne Street. The constable who questioned them had been very kind, and with Lord Everton's testimony of the man he chased from the house, the police soon had all the evidence their small party could provide.

Audra lay awake in her bed several hours more, feeling more vulnerable than ever. Lord Everton had been very kind in escorting them home, but the whiteness of his complexion was a vision that came back to haunt her. Lady Sutherland, too, seemed shaken to the core, to the point her reaction to the whole affair was shockingly silent. Worse still, the authorities speculated the whole event was a crime of passion by one of the lady's many lovers—a theory the jewelry box the lady found beside the body seemed to support.

Audra's conviction that Secret Admirer was the man who murdered Lord Garrington was purely emotional, and she occasionally restrained herself from making her final conclusion by recalling there was a complete lack of motive. After all, she herself had no connection whatsoever to Lord Garrington, and had, in fact, not even been introduced to the man. Audra considered the possibility Secret Admirer had an obsession with ladies other than herself, and that it might indeed have been a crime of passion, but if the authorities were to be believed about the quantity of the lady's amorous partners, they had a string of men to interview. How frustrating when there was likely only one man they needed to find! Audra tossed her pillow over her face and moaned.

Chapter Eight

The next morning, the doorbell rang and Lord Everton was announced. Audra glanced at the clock and was stunned to find he had come before noon.

It was not an unpleasant surprise, though it would have been pleasanter had Audra not been feeling the effects of a sleepless night. Lady Sutherland's panic to meet him in the drawing room brought a throb to Audra's head.

All in all, she was glad of one thing—the last twelve hours had significantly improved her relationship with her patroness, and she marveled how fear had the power to mend. Indeed, the lady's every concern was with Audra's well being. Since the carriage ride home, she had been nothing if not affectionate and reassuring, and her kindness did not dissipate with the morning mist. When the lady met Audra in the morning room for an early breakfast, having passed a similarly sleepless night, she was as genial and motherly as ever. Audra, after having spent the past few weeks feeling very alone and recently terrified, could not but welcome the reassurances of the lady and the peace that comes with forgiveness. After all, she would hear from Thornton *sometime* and in the meanwhile wished not to live with an enemy.

"Dear Lord Everton, how nice to see you this morning." Lady Sutherland vigorously dusted away the crumbs left on her fingers by a flaky cranberry scone to offer him her hand. "Indeed, this is a pleasure."

He smiled broadly. "Lady Sutherland." He tilted his head. "Lady Audra."

"Good morning, Lord Everton," Audra greeted.

"I hope you will forgive me for this early intrusion."

"Intrusion, indeed!" cried Lady Sutherland. "You deserve a hero's welcome, you may rely upon that! Though I, too, must beg your forgiveness, as I was just about to finish a letter to Lord Sutherland for this morning's post. If you'll excuse me, I'm sure Lady Audra can entertain you."

"Of course," he replied.

Thus, Angela Sutherland exited the room as quickly as she had entered it.

"Well, that's very odd," said Audra. "Normally, I cannot get her to leave me alone for two minutes together." She poured herself a cup of rose tea. "Please have a seat. May I offer you some?"

"Thank you," he replied, accepting the invitation as well as the tea.

"We had quite the evening last night, didn't we?" Audra recalled. "I still don't know how to properly thank you."

"Not at all. I only hope my presence is not too powerful a reminder of…well, a frightening situation."

"Lord Everton, don't be ridiculous. It is always a pleasure to see you."

He cast his eyes down to the cup and saucer she held out to him, and Audra thought him a bit nervous. "I am glad to hear you say so, for I have always thought the same of you."

Audra smiled and sipped her tea in her favorite seat near the window. The warm, rose-scented steam was soothing and helped ease her headache.

"So what brings you to Queen Anne Street this morning?"

Lifting his brown eyes to her, he said rather awkwardly, "Well, I've come to see you."

Audra's bell-like laugh danced in the room around them. Under the circumstances, it felt good to laugh at something, even if it was unintentionally humorous.

"Yes, of course. Very good, Lord Everton. If I visit you at your house, I shall say the same."

He chuckled with her. "I suppose that wasn't very clear." The smile quickly faded, and he cleared his throat. "Allow me to be more specific." He tried again, and returning to his previous state of seriousness, said, "I am leaving London this week."

At this, Audra placed down her tea. "Leaving London? Have you come to say goodbye to us, Lord Everton?"

The announcement came as a shock; in fact, the very thought was a blow, and Audra instinctively sat very upright in her chair, as if bracing for bad news, except that it had already been received.

"I was hoping I wouldn't have to," he said, with an awkward inflection and lack of assurance that was unlike him.

Grasping at any small amount of hope he offered, she asked, "So your leaving is uncertain?"

His face was solemn. "My leaving is, indeed, certain. It is only yours that is less so."

"Oh, I am certainly leaving London," she said definitively. "There is no doubt about that."

With this, she lifted her cup and saucer to her lips as if toasting to the plan.

"So you will join me?"

Audra choked on her tea and again set it down on the table beside her. Had she misunderstood him? She fell silent, save for one word. "Join?"

Oh, no, she thought. *No, no, no, no…*

"Join me on my journey? Join me as my wife, Lady Audra."

Audra rose from her seat. "Lord Everton, you mustn't do this."

"I must! Please sit." Respectfully, she sat, her hands gripping the edge of her seat with all her strength. "I am no longer the man you knew on your arrival to London. I am no longer the man who believed any woman would do as a life companion. You have changed me, Lady Audra. My every thought on marriage has been altered because of you. In fact, there is no longer any woman but one who would do."

"Please don't," she whispered.

But he continued, "I never imagined a creature not half my size could hold such power over me. Your exquisite charm has seized my heart, my soul, and my mind, so there is not a beat that does not ache for you, a breath that does not gasp for you, and there is no thought I have been able to master that does not hold you in its wake. I beg you to consider my offer."

"Please, Lord Everton, I beg you, as well. I cherish our friendship. Can we not pretend this conversation never happened and go on just as we have?"

He looked very grave. "I certainly cannot."

"But I cannot accept."

Lord Everton's gaze fell to the floor. Audra squeezed the cushion of her chair. Agonizing silence followed.

"I love you, Audra Kingsley," he said, suddenly. "There. I said it."

How she wished with all her heart that he had not.

"Please understand me," she pleaded, with heartfelt intonation. "You are a wonderful man, Lord Everton. Any woman would be fortunate to have you. But I am not open to any offers."

"You little chit!" Lady Sutherland burst into the room. "Explain yourself, Lady Audra!"

"What?" Audra stared at her in disbelief. "Lady Sutherland— were you *listening*…?"

"Here, at Lord Everton's request, I have arranged for him to speak with you on a very delicate subject, and look at the embarrassment you have caused! Not open to any offers, indeed! Need I remind you this man is your hero?"

"Lady Sutherland, you know that Lord Crispin and I…"

"Oh, hush! When are you ever going to forget him?" she cried. "Lord Everton is the man for you."

Lord Everton stood, reaching for his top hat. "This is most unnecessary, Lady Sutherland. Allow me to gather my things and go in peace."

"Lord Everton," said Audra, at once alert to the necessity of ignoring Lady Sutherland, "I am so very sorry."

He nodded and made his way to the door. "May I ask one thing of you, Lady Audra?"

Disconsolately, she asked, "Yes?"

"As I am leaving town shortly, I would hate this to be our last moment together. I do hope to see you tonight at the Whitehalls' Masquerade Ball. Perhaps we can part with pleasanter memories."

The Whitehalls' Masquerade Ball. Of course it would continue. It had been planned for weeks.

Audra agreed at once. "Of course. I will certainly be there."

"I thank you." Addressing Lady Sutherland, Lord Everton said, as if scolding a child, "Please do not discuss this further once I am gone."

Lady Sutherland opened her mouth as if to say something, but decided against it. Satisfied, Lord Everton took his leave, closing the door behind him. With equal swiftness, Lady Sutherland stormed out of the drawing room, leaving Audra to the eyes of a handful of servants.

• • •

Devastation and fear. They were the only emotions Audra was capable of feeling as she sat at the edge of her bedroom window. The masquerade ball was only a few hours away, and all she could do at this lonely hour was wait in silent, miserable dread.

Lord Everton's proposal, and her subsequent refusal, accounted for the devastation. Surely, she had lost one of her only friends in London, and her already fragile emotions at being trapped in the city were more heavily frayed. She wondered at her own accountability. Had she given him the wrong idea? Had she flirted with him? Had she given him reason to hope? Certainly, she was very comfortable with him. Each time the questions arose, she felt convinced she had been firm with him that she was to marry Crispin, but the questions continued to plague her.

Secret Admirer accounted for the fear. Lord Everton may have frightened him off for the time being, and she doubted he would make an appearance out in the open. But a masquerade? What prevented a masked madman from seeking her out yet again, under the cover of a disguise? And if he was, indeed, a murderer… Audra shuddered. That the ball would be a private affair, held at the home of another of her father's long-time friends, the Whitehalls, was her only reassurance, but not knowing Secret Admirer's name or connections, she knew it was entirely possible for him to be invited. If she had not promised Lord Everton she would attend, she would have avoided it at all costs.

Audra flatly refused to accompany Lady Sutherland to tea that afternoon with a group of ladies that included Lady DeBlock and Embeth. After Lady Sutherland's atrocious outburst that morning in front of Lord Everton, Audra was quite over forgiving her, and in no position to attempt graciousness to the lady even in the presence of others. Lady Sutherland, with a shockingly innocent and surprised air, went away with nothing but Audra's excuse of a headache.

Molly, like the rest of the servants, had heard the whole of the morning's scene, and responded very feelingly toward this and all of Audra's experiences as of late. Audra had no doubt Molly would have remained with her, if she had asked. But Audra did not ask. For now, Audra was content to sit alone in her chamber, her legs curled up underneath her on the windowsill, and her head pressed against the glass.

With so much weighing on her mind and heart, Audra allowed herself a moment to close her eyes, and even hoped to drift off.

After all, in sleep she would not feel the frustration, the worry, the loneliness. But her anxiety did not allow her to do so, and she was soon on her feet, pacing her room. She swung gently around her bedposts; she walked circles around her writing desk. Molly had hung her gold and ivory gown outside the closet, and though the details were lost on her at the moment, she ran her fingers along the ruffles. Her white lace and pearl mask sat on her dresser beside her pearl necklace, gloves, and Crispin's baby portrait.

Desperate for a diversion, Audra turned her attention to the reticule Molly had laid out and decided it was not the one she wanted to use this night. It was not that it was not pretty, and it was not that it did not match. It was simply that everything about her outfit, from the dress to the mask, had been purchased in London. There was not an item to be worn that had come from home.

And she so wished to be near home.

Audra opened the closet and rummaged through her things. Pulling a small, ivory reticule from one of the shelves, she smiled at it—a gift from Rhianna. She rose and held it up to her gown. She smiled at the perfect match and made her way to her vanity, contented to switch her personal items from one reticule to another.

The sight of a folded letter in the creases of the bag from home brought a gasp to Audra's lips. Fear took over, and she dropped the reticule to the ground. How long had the letter been there? Audra did not recall using this particular reticule since her arrival in London. She wondered frantically if Secret Admirer had broken into her home. And what was more, why bury a letter so deeply away in an object hidden in the back of a closet? Why not somewhere more obvious, more visible, more likely to be found?

Time seemed to crawl to a stop as she glared at the limp reticule, its singular item seeming to have a life of its own. Audra half expected it to jump out at her at any moment. The reticule itself, once a cherished gift from a beloved sister, seemed forever tainted.

"Oh," she cried aloud, "stop being ridiculous!"

Audra snatched the reticule from the floor and seized the letter. Tossing the bag aside, she walked to the window. She hesitated before unveiling the article in her clenched fingers. Blast this man for frightening her so! She drew courage from anger and looked at the inscription on the cover.

To Audra.

She hesitated. Had the inscription read, *Lady Audra*, or *My Dearest*, or even, *My Pet*, the fear would have intensified, and she would have felt it rise in her throat with a sick, choking sensation. But there was something different about this particular inscription.

"To Audra," she read aloud.

And there was something else. The handwriting. It was neater. And the ink. It left no smudges, no blotches. Even the lines themselves, though a man's writing, were finer, not written with a hard hand.

Audra felt her heart quicken, but not with fear. She knew this handwriting, yes, *loved* this handwriting. It was *Crispin's* handwriting!

She nearly tore it as she unfolded it, her eyes eager to devour the words he had delivered to her. She knew not at what point he had written them, or at what point he hoped she would find them, but rejoiced that she had found them now, in one of her darkest hours. And with a still breath, she read:

> Dear Audra,
>
> I thought it best to write to you now, before I am in the depths of despair, and no sooner have I written those words than I realize I am already there. You may not have left Thornton, and as of this note, I will still see you once more before you do so, but your impending departure and the subsequent event of our insufferable

separation looms thick and heavy in the air to the point I find myself fighting for breath.

But my intention in writing you is not to speak of the unbearable feelings of being severed from you, or the unendurable thoughts that haunt me of the men in London whose attentions you will undoubtedly receive, welcomed or not. Rather, I wish you to be assured beyond a shadow of a doubt that I, Crispin Brighton, am wholly, unquestionably, and emphatically yours. I suspect you already know this, and have known this, these last four years, but I can think of no instance in which a declaration that you and I belong together can be said too often. And there is no distance on this Earth or in the realms above so great that could tear my devotion from you, so what are a few hundred miles to us? I will wait for your return, however impatiently, with growing affection and loyal commitment to our future life together.

You may credit my dear sister-in-law, Rhianna, with slipping this into your reticule for me. It is for such actions as these that she becomes dearer to me every day, as my own flesh and blood.

I love you, Audra. I have loved you forever, and I will love you forever.

Yours, Crispin

She pressed the note to her heart. Too emotional even for tears, she made her way to the bed, crawled up with the blessed note, and kissed it.

• • •

Audra sat numbly at her vanity, her ivory and gold masquerade gown making her one with the furniture of the room. She examined her ivory skirts, the intermittent horizontal ruffles cascading around her, and the gold overlay and flared sleeves trimmed with bows. She ran her fingers down the bullion ruffles running vertically down the center of her bodice and wished Crispin could see her once the finishing touches had been applied. Her white, shimmering mask, decorated with pearls and white feathers that sprang upward from a single pearl brocade placed between the brows, was just one such final touch. It went very nicely with her pearl jewelry, and she thought briefly that, of all the dinner parties, balls, and gatherings she had been to, this at least was the most interesting.

Molly pinned her hair silently. Audra watched her through the mirror, sensing something was troubling her. She liked Molly. She was a quiet girl, but friendly, and she never complained. Audra had vented to her frequently over the weeks at her frustration of wanting to go home, and Molly had been an understanding, kind ear to her.

"Molly," Audra addressed, "are you all right this evening?"

The attention brought upon her startled the lady's maid, and she turned anxious, brown eyes on Audra. "I do beg your pardon, miss?"

Audra felt that Molly pinned her hair more furiously, and asked, "What is troubling you?"

Molly shook her head and adjusted Audra's curls silently.

"You're not telling me something," Audra said, watching Molly's expression in the mirror change from concern to one of fear. "What is it?"

Stilling her fingers around Audra's curls, Molly shot her a pleading look. "Lady Audra, if I get dismissed, I'd have nowhere to go." After a pause, she added, "If I tell you what I've seen, would you promise me not to let it leave this room?"

Audra was at the height of alarm. If whatever Molly had witnessed was bad enough to get her dismissed, Audra must know of it. She rose from the seat of the vanity, and taking Molly by the hands, led her to the edge of bed where she sat beside her.

"Molly," Audra assured, "whatever it is you have seen, I will personally see to it that you are protected, even rewarded for exposing something improper that is happening in this house."

"I believe you would," said Molly, nodding. "I've wanted to tell you something for a while, but I was so afraid."

"Well, you're doing the right thing by telling me now," Audra encouraged. "Now, what is it you have seen?"

Molly took a deep breath. "Lady Sutherland," she began hesitantly. "It's to do with Lady Sutherland."

Audra felt her muscles stiffen, but patted Molly's hands encouragingly. "Yes?"

Then, in a sentence that came so swiftly it might have been heard as a single word, she said, "I've seen her burning things."

Burning?

Audra ignored the echoing word in her mind and tried to look as nonchalant and approachable as possible.

"What sorts of things?" Audra aided.

Molly turned troubled eyes upon her, her hands shivering and clammy. "Letters."

Audra straightened her back and squared her shoulders. "Letters?" she repeated.

"Aye."

"Molly," said Audra, fighting with all her might to speak with a slow, calm-sounding voice, "do I understand you correctly? Did you just say that Lady Sutherland is *burning letters?*"

Seeming fearful, Molly nodded. "William collects them as they come in, and he gives them to her."

"William, the butler?" Audra asked, her muscles tense, blood boiling in her veins.

"Lady Audra, please, I don't want to get in trouble. I beg for your protection."

With this, Molly dropped her face in her hands and sobbed. The moment caught Audra by surprise, but she rested a reassuring hand on Molly's shoulder.

"Molly, you are a faithful, honest servant. I swear to you, when I am married to Lord Crispin, I will request you personally as my lady's maid at Kingsley Manor."

"Ooh!" she cried, taken aback. "That would be too generous, surely."

"Nothing is too generous for a trustworthy house servant, Molly. Now, please, tell me everything."

Molly nodded again, growing braver, and her eyes growing dryer. "I first saw her burn a letter only a few days after you arrived. After, I watched her closely. William collects them from the doorman, gives them to Lady Sutherland, and she tosses each one of them into the fire when she thinks no one is looking, one by one."

"Did she read them?"

"Oh, yes."

"How many letters has she burned?" Audra managed, fighting to hide her infuriation before Molly.

"Oh, batches of them. More than I could count."

Audra bit down on her tongue before speaking again. "Before these letters were burned, did you ever…did you happen to see who they were from?"

Molly shook her head. "No I…Well, I can't read very well. I did try to collect fragments from the ashes to give to you directly, but all was burned to a crisp."

"That was very good of you, Molly," Audra commended; surprised to hear she had taken this extra step. "I am much pleased by your efforts."

Molly thanked her. "Lady Audra, I know you suspect these letters were from Thornton, but before you condemn Lady Sutherland completely, there is one other possibility."

Audra was staring off in thought toward the far wall of her bedchamber. "*Mmm*?" she managed.

"William caught me at the fireplace trying to collect the burnt letters. He said, 'It's none of our business if Lady Sutherland has a lover'."

This snapped her back to reality, and she turned a sharp eye on Molly. "A lover?"

As she said it, Audra doubted not that Lady Sutherland could have a lover. It only seemed odd that she would burn the letters if they were, in fact, from him. Did not women keep and cherish letters from lovers? On the other hand, had Audra not written multiple letters to multiple recipients at Thornton without receiving a single response?

Molly hesitated before adding, "I don't know that I believe him. I suspect Lady Sutherland gives William a bit of money in exchange for the letters."

After assuring Molly that her confession was appreciated and that she should not worry about the matter any further, they returned to the dresser to complete Audra's hair for the masquerade. They spoke little after this, as Molly recuperated from her divulgence, and Audra considered all possible reasons Lady Sutherland might have for destroying communication from anyone.

•••

The masquerade had raised Lady Sutherland's usual excitement to new heights, and she spoke animatedly of the event as they traveled to the Whitehalls', where the private affair was being held. Indeed, she spoke to Audra as if the morning's event with Lord Everton had never occurred—never mind a murder the evening before.

As Lady Sutherland chatted on, the very thought of her having schemed or hidden anything from Thornton seemed outrageous to Audra. Lady Sutherland was a decidedly silly woman, whom Audra was quite sure had not the least idea that Audra had been slighting her these last weeks. And despite the lady's stubborn determination to remain in London, she seemed incapable of such deception—not to mention, Audra found her devoid of motive. Perhaps it *was* a lover's letters, and perhaps it was a lover that kept her in London. Audra thought that keeping one eye on Lady Sutherland's company this night, and one eye out for Secret Admirer, would keep her sufficiently busy for one evening.

Lord and Lady Whitehall met them just inside the door of their rectangular, red brick mansion, and despite their masks recognized Audra and Lady Sutherland at once. Audra knew she would be as visible as ever to someone looking for her, but standing beside the boisterous Lady Sutherland made her doubly recognizable. She vowed to escape her the moment she could, and was soon rescued by Embeth's Lord Wesley.

He escorted her to the dance floor where an excitable crowd had gathered. Perhaps they hoped to hurry the musicians as they tuned their instruments. One thing was certain: they all seemed very ready to have a good time despite the previous night's events. And though murder seemed the only topic of conversation, the general mood of the crowd was very happy, indeed.

The ballroom itself was lovely, illuminated by thousands of candles on wall mounts, candelabrums, and three enormous chandeliers. A local florist had been hired to decorate the room in such a way as to give the appearance of a garden, and despite the overwhelming fragrance, the resulting atmosphere was so lovely, one's nose was willing to forgive the heavy aroma for the beauty left to the eyes.

"Embeth has not yet arrived, I take it?" Audra asked Lord Wesley, smiling.

"Not yet," he said with an awkward shyness. "Miss DeBlock means to play a fine trick on me by hiding in her mask, but I told her I'd spot her right away."

"I am sure you will," Audra told him.

The dancing began. They separated while she considered he was a nice boy, and with Lord Everton leaving London with a broken heart, Audra was prepared to accept Lord Wesley as her dear friend's future husband.

"I do hope you will propose to her soon," she told him as they came back together. "I will be married as soon as I can get home, and I so want you and Embeth to be among our first dinner guests at Kingsley Manor."

Lord Wesley's mouth fell agape, and he tripped over his own feet.

"Well, you mean to, don't you?" Audra pressed shamelessly. "You know she'll say yes, and—Lord Wesley, if you break her heart, so help me…"

"Please, oh, Lady Audra, dear me, if you would just, oh…" He looked around them as if the decorative, marble lions were preying upon him from every angle, then he glanced back at Audra, to the crowds, then back at Audra. Then, in a cautious voice, loud enough only for Audra to hear through the music, he asked, "Do you really think she would say yes?"

Audra grinned widely. "Yes, you silly! You should ask her tonight and not waste anymore time. It'll make her wildly happy."

He bared horse-like teeth at her, despite a fine effort to purse his lips closed over his large, awkward mouth, and thus Audra was assured of her newfound friendship with Lord Wesley. He might not have been a handsome man, but Embeth was sure to get exactly what she wanted with him—a trustworthy and loyal husband. Audra liked him the better for it.

It was a pleasant moment in the night, and she was grateful to him for it.

•••

Half past the stroke of midnight, Audra was standing in the tea-room of the Whitehalls' home when she caught a glimpse of the unmistakable salt-and-pepper hair of Secret Admirer. She froze just long enough to see him turn his half-masked face to meet her gaze. Audra bolted out the door, pushing through a sea of costumed guests, and she did not turn back to see if he followed.

Turning a quick corner, and then another, she stole up a staircase with the distinct sensation of having someone at her heels. There was no time to consider her actions as she entered the first room she came across.

Without a moment's hesitation, she made her way through a maze of walnut furniture to ginger-colored curtains that draped floor-to-ceiling windows. Tossing the thick material aside, she slid behind it, pulling her skirts tight to her sides.

A faint pair of footsteps sounded in the hallway and then continued on. Audra closed her eyes, listening as the sound distanced and faded into nothing.

Her relief was short-lived. Moments after, footsteps louder and more determined sounded in the hall.

Audra held her breath as the door opened, and a voice cried, "Come out from there! Do you think you can hide from me?"

Audra dug her fingernails into the marbled turquoise wallpaper behind her. Dare she step out from behind the curtain? Secret Admirer may have seen her enter the room, but there was at least one other exit. Or were there two? He could have no reason to think she would not have escaped through one of them. Pressing her small body against the wall, she held her breath; still convinced her hiding place was not positively compromised.

"Do not try my patience. I said, come out!"

The voice had a fear-inducing effect so paralyzing that all she could do was clench her teeth and shut her eyes. Her body stood frozen, her feet planted to the floor by her satin slippers. Tremors shook her soul as she anticipated his approach and imagined him tugging the heavy drapery away from before her.

Suddenly, there was a rustling beside her. Audra started as the voice of a young girl spoke.

"Do not be angry with me, Uncle Harry," she pleaded.

Uncle Harry?

Audra connected the voice to the ten-year-old niece of Lord Harold Whitehall, in whose house Audra was now a guest. And the man she spoke to—why, now that she thought about it, his voice was nothing like Secret Admirer's. Just as she connected the voice to Lord Whitehall, Audra realized Secret Admirer had not followed her into the study at all!

Despite this relief, the sound of fabric brushing against fabric startled Audra further as she listened to her fellow curtain dweller answer Lord Whitehall's call to come out.

"It is not so easy to go to sleep when there is a party in the house," the young girl confessed.

"Even so," Lord Whitehall told her sternly, "parties are for big girls. Your day will come. Get along, then, and do not have me chasing you all about the house."

"Yes, uncle."

Their feet shuffled, a doorknob was turned, and they were gone.

Audra exhaled strongly, grabbing her midriff as the door closed behind them. She was grateful her presence had not been revealed, and she had no explaining to do to Lord Whitehall, who undoubtedly would have demanded answers to questions he had every right to ask.

Audra tripped out from behind the curtain and fell into an oversized chair. It was a man's study, she noted before allowing her head to fall to the side of the seat's wing as she caught her breath. It was a difficult task. Corsets, after all, were not designed to allow young ladies running from obsessive secret admirers to catch their breath. She twisted in discomfort.

"Do you make it a habit of hiding behind drapery, Lady Audra?"

With a start, Audra leapt to her feet and met a man, his face hidden by a black, Venetian mask that covered the whole of his face. It was not one of the diagonal half-masks popular among the men, but it was clear from the lack of gray in his dark hair that he was not Secret Admirer.

Where he had come from, she did not know, but Audra breathed a sigh of relief. "Oh! Thank God you're not him."

The masked man cocked his head to the side. "Him?"

Audra dropped her white lace and feathered mask and twirled it by its handle toward the window. "The reason I was hiding behind the curtains."

Pressing the fingers of his black leather gloves together in a thoughtful gesture, he noted, "It sounds as if you have an interesting story to tell."

Audra peered at him. "Do I know you? Or do you intend to keep your mask in place for the remainder of our conversation?"

"I think the question is not whether or not you know me," he countered, "but whether or not have we been properly introduced. If we have not, it would be very inappropriate for me to be speaking with you at this moment, and I do rather wish to speak to you. There is something fascinating about a person who has just emerged from behind a curtain."

Audra narrowed her eyes further. "And if we *have* been introduced?"

"If we have been introduced, Lady Audra," he humored, "than by retaining my mask, my objective must simply be to keep my identity a secret and you in blind suspense."

Amused, Audra was willing to accept his position. "I can see you are not particularly inclined to remove it," she said. "Well, there is only one person whose presence I could do without, and seeing as how you are not him…"

"You seem very certain."

"Well," she allowed, "if you count my patroness, then there are *two* persons I could do without, but you are clearly not a lady."

The masked man took a seat in a great, red chair and held out his hand to the couch beside him, signaling her to sit. "So, then. You *do* have an interesting story to tell. Would you tell it to a masked stranger?"

Would she, indeed?

Audra followed the direction of his outstretched hand, seated herself, and smoothed her skirts. "Desperate times…Yes, I believe I would. One never knows where help might come from."

Crossing one leg over the other, the masked man leaned forward in a posture of keen attention, and echoed, "Help?"

Audra took an uncomfortably deep breath. *Here goes nothing*, she thought.

"I am being kept in London against my will," she said.

It felt good to say it, and to say it so brusquely, for fury she had not known she suppressed bubbled to the surface with her words, and as they spilled from her lips she felt some relief. He sat silent. Surprisingly so, Audra thought, considering the severity of her language.

She continued, "Now, I have a secret admirer who might be a murderer, and I just want to go home!"

This last sentence seemed to fall out rather haphazardly, but Audra had little concern with giving her tale in a neat and tidy package.

He nodded, slowly. "Where is home?"

Home. There was no other word that dripped with such delightful sweetness.

"Thornton," she said, the pain in her heart reverberating in her voice. "It meets the cliffs of the North Sea. Do you know it?"

"I've heard of it," said the voice from behind the mask. "Why do you not write home and have someone come for you?"

Outrage rose high in her breast and she took to her feet. "You think me a fool?"

"Please, do sit back down."

"You think I have not thought to write?" she cried. "Well, I *have* written. Many times. And I have heard nothing in return."

Though she was generally not one for tears, Audra's eyes stung as she spoke. She closed them momentarily and then turned them back on her companion.

The masked man appeared to look down at his hands for some time before he returned her gaze. Again, he asked her to sit, and for the kindness in his tone, she obliged him.

"Why do you suppose they have not responded?" he asked.

Silence hung in the air following this question. During her weeks in London, it was a question she had turned over in her mind again and again. It was only because of Molly's confession earlier that day Audra felt she might have a theory.

"I suspect…"

Audra paused before placing accusations against her patroness. It was bad enough she had said as much as she had to a man who hid his identity. If only he had not put her so at ease! Once again, her comfort level had placed her in danger of speaking too freely.

"Oh, but I wish I knew," she said, her voice a whisper as a choking feeling gripped her throat.

"Lady Audra," said he, "I am in no rush to return to the night's festivities. Why do you not start at the beginning?"

• • •

She did not know how much time had passed once she completed her tale, only that the masked stranger listened attentively and with little interruption. At his bid to start at the beginning, she told him of her father's wish for her to be presented at St. James, her expectations of leaving London within a week of arrival, and

Lady Sutherland's subsequent refusal. Audra realized for the first time that despite Lady Sutherland's claims of having friends and family in London to visit, Audra had met no family of hers during their weeks in London, and they had spent little time with anyone beyond Embeth and her mother. What was more, Lady DeBlock did not seem a long-time friend of Lady Sutherland's at all, but rather a distant contact whose acquaintance had been renewed only this Season. In fact, Lady DeBlock did not even seem particularly fond of Lady Sutherland, but appeared only to tolerate her because Audra and Embeth liked each other so well.

Without offering the gentleman's name, she told the masked stranger of Lord Everton, and how she had broken his heart by refusing his proposal of marriage even after telling him time and again not to fall in love with her. And, of course, there was Secret Admirer to discuss, and Audra shivered as she recalled how that unfortunate tale turned out. She vehemently told her masked companion how she did not want Secret Admirer's love notes, and had he given her any opportunity to speak with him at all, she would have told him from the start of her beloved Lord Crispin.

When she was finished, she buried her face in her hands and breathed deeply. She waited, but the masked man said nothing. Suddenly, turning her head up, she looked feverishly about the room until her eyes fell upon the prize she craved. With a leap, she was off the couch, opening a cabinet and pulling out a bottle of brandy from its recesses. Reaching also for a glass, she turned to offer one to her companion and was surprised to find him standing beside her.

"Audra," he said, reaching for the bottle.

She pulled it back, but the change in his voice stunned her, and recognizing it as one she knew well, she did not refuse the brandy to him when his fingers encompassed it.

"Who are you?" she asked, and her fingers loosened around the glass she yet held.

The masked stranger took the glass also from her and placed both brandy and glass on a round table beside them. He took a step toward her, but she responded with a step back. Placing her hand upon his breast to keep him at bay, she froze. The masked stranger's heart pulsated wildly beneath her palm. Instinctively, Audra withdrew her hand, but he quickly seized it with his own and pressed it firmly to his chest.

"I had lost all hope, Audra. I thought you were gone forever."

She gasped as the full disguise of his voice was dropped and she examined the ice-blue eyes that met hers from behind the black Venetian mask.

"Can you be real?" she breathed.

With his free hand, Crispin pulled the mask up over his face and let it drop to the oriental rug. Allowing herself only a moment's luxury of looking at his revealed face, Audra flung her body against his, and he tightened his arms around her. As she melted into him and pressed her face into the folds of his ruffled, white shirt, the sudden release of emotions brought a flood of tears to her eyes, and she sobbed unashamedly into the stiff linen.

Soon, comforting fingers stroked her shoulders and neck, and with her face still pressed against his lapel, she lifted her eyes to him.

"Crispin."

And with that single word, all power went out of her. The strength with which she threw herself at him drained from every muscle with the pull of a myriad of emotions, and he caught her as she stumbled under weak knees.

Crispin assisted her back to the couch and sat beside her, removing his gloves to stroke her arms, her shoulders, and to run loving fingers along the sides of her face. She found herself staring at him, wondering if her vision was playing tricks on her, or if retelling her experiences from the last few weeks had overwhelmed her into delirium.

"Why did no one come for me?" she managed at last. "Why did no one write?"

Crispin pressed his forehead to hers and shook his head. "We did not get any of your letters, Audra." His voice began to sound far away as she heard him tell her, "Breathe slower, Audra. Slow and deep."

He pressed her head into his shoulder, and he held it there securely. Audra closed her eyes and tried to obey his instructions, pressing her hand to his thigh for support. He stiffened slightly, but did not protest.

"Lady Sutherland said you were remaining in London for the Season," he told her.

The words were distant to her ears, but they were not lost on her. "You received letters from Lady Sutherland, but not from me?"

She felt him rock her gently, and she enjoyed the soothing motion. "She sent two letters, weeks apart. Audra, you have no idea the frustration I have felt…"

"How is it that you are you here?"

"When I told Lord Whitehall I was coming to London, he invited me to stay here. He knew, of course, that you were here, and that the townhouse was unavailable to me. He told me you would be at the masquerade tonight."

"I am *so* glad you have come." Pushing herself back to look at him, she asked, "Did anyone else come with you?"

Crispin shook his head. "I came alone, after Lady Sutherland's last, vague letter. You have to understand; we were all under the impression you wanted to be here. Lady Sutherland…"

"Oh! Her very name is offensive. I have reason to believe she has been interfering with our communication. What did she write?"

Crispin produced a note, which read, in part:

…You really must excuse dear Lady Audra for not writing directly. She comes home so tired from parties; she simply collapses into her bedchamber…she knows I will write you as often as possible. Of course, we expect the coming weeks to be as busy as ever…

"She is a liar!" Audra said sharply. She handed it back to him, unable to read further. "She knew I wrote to you. I questioned her about not receiving any communication from home. My maidservant, Molly, told me she witnessed Lady Sutherland burning letters. She must have been burning mine as well as yours."

Crispin shook his head. "I knew something was strange from the very first."

"I don't know why she wants to keep me here," Audra continued, "but Crispin, I always intended to come home. I promised you I would come home. You do believe me, don't you?"

"Shh," he eased her. "We're going to go home. Together. Tonight."

The question of how this was to be done never made it from her parted lips. His own had not been against hers for some time, and Crispin spread a series of soft kisses from one corner of her mouth to the other. Four years she had been kissing these lips, and for four years they had been sending shivers through her body. A rush of heat spread from her core as he pulled her closer, his warm breath swirling in her open mouth.

"You still give me butterflies, Audra," he confessed, forcing some distance between them.

Reality soon came back to her. "Crispin, you know it would be scandalous for us to ride alone together. Ought you not to write to Lord Brighton and request he meet us here?"

"Why wait? I can rent a coach. If you would be willing to wear some of my clothes, we could avoid detection and be in Thornton by the end of the week."

"Wear your—do you mean I should dress as a *boy*?" she asked.

"You should be the prettiest boy I've ever seen," he told her. "Of course, if you strongly object…"

"I most certainly do not! Let us get to Thornton as soon as possible!"

Crispin smiled broadly. "I will gather the clothes now and bring them to the townhouse before you and Lady Sutherland return home tonight. Who do you think it best to leave them with?"

"Molly," Audra answered confidently. "Leave them with Molly, and she will see to it that Lady Sutherland never knows what we are planning."

"And I'll pick you up just before sunrise."

She nodded, and with these plans in place, they fell silent. Crispin held her face in the palms of his hands, and she watched as he examined her every feature. Neither attempted to describe what they had suffered, for they each had felt it; they each already knew.

"Let's not go," said Audra in a drained voice. "Not just yet."

It seemed an unnecessary request, as Crispin showed himself in no hurry to part with her.

"You've never looked so beautiful," he whispered, running the tips of his fingers along her eyebrows, eyelashes, nose, and lips. "Can you be real?"

She recalled her sentiment of earlier as he brushed his knuckles across her cheeks and down the curve of her neck. Then, plucking the chain from her throat, he lifted his gold promise ring from within her bodice and examined it with a smile.

Overcome, Audra leaned against him, pressing her bosom against his ruffled shirt, and Crispin allowed the weight of her torso to push him against the corner of the sofa. Using her hand upon his thigh, she propelled herself up, running the tip of her nose along his neck in search of his smell. The weeks she had spent denied of his scent made her crave it, and now, finding herself suddenly enveloped, she was excessively greedy of it. Desiring not only to smell the sacred aroma but to absorb it, she drew a long breath through her open mouth, tasting the concentrated bouquet on her tongue. She drew in his sweet air until her corset allowed nothing further and then postponed exhaling until she could no longer hold her breath. The warmth that rose from his skin carried the intoxicating fragrance to her with overpowering force and with it a wave of desire down her spine, around her ribs, and down her legs.

As if this sudden and intense rush were visible to the naked eye, Crispin locked her body against his with one unyielding arm. His free hand cupped the back of her neck, drawing her closer to him, his fingers combing into the hair of her bun. Their eyes met, and a tempest of emotions overtook her, a powerful mixture of love, passion, and safety.

"Will you marry me, Audra?"

"So the world can see the commitment I have already made in my heart? Yes."

Crispin pulled her closer, and their lips merged. At last, nothing was left but to obtain her father's permission—a simple formality, really—and she would be engaged to her Crispin.

Officially.

• • •

Embeth wore such a worried look in every muscle around her eyes and mouth that Audra poked her.

"Don't look so conspicuous!" she cried. "I'm telling you so you *don't* worry. Not a word, do you hear me? Not *one word* to anyone. Swear it."

"Swear? Oh, Audra, how unbecoming…"

"You have to do it."

"Can I not just promise?"

"No."

"Oh! Very well, Audra, I *swear*. Of course I do."

"Good." Audra took Embeth's hands in hers. "I will write to you once I'm home. We'll see each other again soon. You must come to Thornton."

"Audra," Embeth said hurriedly. "I shall have to bring Lord Wesley." Audra looked at her, a smile traveling across her face. "He has proposed," Embeth confirmed happily. "And I have accepted him, obviously!"

Audra offered her heartiest congratulations. "Now we are both on our way down the aisle. How perfect!" With a final squeeze of Embeth's hands, she said, "I must go."

As she began to dart off, Embeth called, "Audra, whatever has happened to your hair?"

Audra simply smiled, and remembering the fine mess Crispin had made of it, hurried her fingers to her head for the escaped strands.

Chapter Nine

"Molly, close the door!" Audra's fingers tugged at the few loophole buttons she could reach at the back of her dress. "He is early!"

The shadow of the black carriage outside the drawing room window, with its swinging lanterns and dark horses, left her more breathless than her flight up the stairs to her chamber. Oh! Whatever was the time? She prayed Lady Sutherland had fallen asleep as Molly hurried to assist with the removal of her gown. At the same time, Audra dragged Crispin's brown leather bag across the bed toward her by the strap. With one fluid gesture, the bag was opened and the clothing lay strewn across the quilt. She eyed the ruffled white shirt, starkly bright against the black breeches, vest, jacket, and hat, and tapped her feet anxiously until Molly urged her to be still. At long last, they were pulling her gown down from her shoulders, and not a moment too soon, for Audra was quite ready to take a pair of scissors to the material. Stepping over the fabrics ballooning about her waist, Audra tripped out of her gown, and taking the bedpost with one hand, grabbed for Crispin's white shirt with the other.

Molly reached to undo her corset, but Audra waved her away. "There is no time," she said. "The pants, Molly, quickly!"

One leg, then the other, and Audra was tightening the loose pants around her tiny waist with the last hole of Crispin's belt. In almost the same moment, her arms were through the vest, and Audra was pushing gold buttons through the holes of the double-breasted jacket.

"Molly, my bags!" said Audra, tucking her curls under the top hat, wanting Crispin to have the full effect of the costume upon first sight of her.

Molly brought two bags to the bedchamber door, and Audra took them by the handles. "You get the others," Audra instructed, and she left for the stairs.

• • •

Audra walked briskly but silently toward the front door, hardly aware that light now filled the drawing room.

"Lady Audra."

She stopped, wondering if it was the sound of her name or the woman's voice that called it that halted her. It was no matter now that Lady Sutherland was awake, she told herself. She could not prevent her from leaving with Crispin now. She was dressed, her bags were packed, and Crispin waited for her just outside. She turned back to Molly, who stood at the top of the stairs, and waved her back. There was no need to incriminate her in this scheme. She would spare a moment for Lady Sutherland before getting her own things with Crispin's help.

Placing her bags down at the front door, Audra made her way to the threshold of the drawing room. "Lady Sutherland."

Audra met her patroness's sharp gaze from across the room with her shoulders squared, her mouth set, and her chin held high as a sign of her determination. There could be no mistaking her intentions, she was sure, and she had no interest in hiding them.

"That is quite an outfit," Lady Sutherland stated coldly from the comfort of her favorite yellow chair. "The tailor was not very good, I think."

Audra held the lady's gaze and, matching the iciness of her voice, said, "No doubt your observations have extended beyond my clothing to the carriage that waits for me."

"Oh, yes," she said, and Audra noted a frosty inflection never before used by the lady. "I did notice."

A silence fell over them, and each examined the other.

"Where were you tonight?" Lady Sutherland asked. "You were nowhere to be found for the majority of the evening. I would have liked to have seen you try a little harder to ease poor Lord Everton's broken heart."

To Audra, this seemed a silly matter to bring up at this juncture, a subject that would have been better suited to the carriage ride home from the Whitehalls'. As she gripped the doorframe with angry fingers, weeks of frustration at being kept in London at Lady Sutherland's hand flushed over her.

With a burst of emotion, Audra said, "I am sorry you had hopes of marrying me off to whomever you deemed acceptable, but my life with Crispin was set long before I came here with you."

Lady Sutherland's face took on a strange look—the look of one who has been caught formulating a sinister plot, and who, without time to decide on a reaction, offers none.

"I will not be your entertainment anymore, Lady Sutherland," Audra continued. "You will have to find another young debutante to marry off."

Audra turned toward the door, wondering at the sound of steps chasing up after her. Whatever Lady Sutherland thought she would do to stop her, Audra did not know. She turned to face her after twisting the handle of the door and pulling it toward her.

Audra gasped as a swift, wide hand—a man's hand—reached over her shoulder and shoved the door closed. Her eyes turned upward, and her breathing was stilled by the vision of a broad, manly frame beside her, his one arm extending over her and his hand pressed firmly against the door. Audra met the face of a man she had not been introduced to during her time in London, but a man she recognized. A man she had hoped she would never see again.

Secret Admirer.

Fear closed up her airways, and though she wanted desperately to scream, she couldn't. Her lungs tightened against her racing heart, and seeing the opportunity to flee from his side into the drawing room, she took it.

Lady Sutherland remained seated in her yellow chair. "There is no time. Make it quick," she said blandly to Secret Admirer.

The man followed Audra, but only so far as the doorway. With her back to the wall of the drawing room and her eyes upon him, Audra inched toward the window. Feeling the paneling against her fingers, she stole a quick glance outside. There, through the pre-dawn darkness, she caught her breath again as the shadow of a man emerged from the carriage and walked toward the door.

Crispin.

Moments later, a knock sounded, then the turning of the handle, and finally the sound of footsteps. Audra thanked heaven Secret Admirer did not turn his gaze away from her. She waited and watched for Crispin to appear. Her eyes longed to see him, for she was sure the sight of him would give her strength not only to regain her voice, but to press away from the wall and leave Queen Anne Street under his protection.

As she heard the door close, a chilling thought came to her: What if Secret Admirer resorted to physical conflict? As quickly as the thought came to her, she dismissed it. Secret Admirer, though tall, was old; Crispin was young and strong. If need be, she was certain Crispin could overpower him. Of course, she hoped such thoughts of combat were hers and hers alone.

"It seems it is time for you to go," Lady Sutherland said to her casually. Audra flashed her patroness a look of disgust before returning her gaze to the door, where Secret Admirer began to step aside. "I expect one day we shall meet again."

Audra hoped not, but didn't trouble herself to say so. Her hand clutched her waist and she wondered what was taking Crispin so long to appear. Finally, she could bear the wait no longer. Audra exhaled a deep breath and, with Crispin's name on her lips, she bolted toward the hallway.

"Audra!"

She had run into Lord Everton before she realized it was him standing in the hall. With her forearms resting against his chest and her mouth agape, she looked at him blankly. When his arms closed over her, she wanted to feel some relief, but there was only confusion.

"Secret Admirer," she managed, finding her voice for the first time since the dreaded man had appeared.

Lord Everton's eyes were dark, and she thought he returned her gaze with difficulty. "Yes," he said, slowly. "Yes, I know." He hurried, "There is no reason to worry. I shall explain everything."

Audra drew a breath, a question rising on her lips as a hand from behind placed a rag over her nose and mouth.

And everything went dark.

• • •

"Thayne?" Crispin was nothing short of shocked to see his elder brother drive up to the Queen Anne Street townhouse in a hired coach. "What in God's name…?"

"You're here!" Thayne called out the window, a strong sense of relief in his voice. He jumped out of the vehicle, paid the driver, and instructed him to drive on. "I was prepared to search all the inns of London for you if you weren't."

"Chasing after me, are you?" Crispin asked as his brother entered his own, hired cab. The opened door brought a draft of cool morning air, and Crispin rolled his shoulders, shaking a sudden chill from them. "Well, it's a good thing I came to London, brother. As it turns out, Lady Sutherland has been keeping Audra here against her will."

"Yes, I suspected as much," he said, shutting the door.

Crispin locked his gaze upon him. "Is that so? You didn't suspect as much when I left."

Thayne examined the face of the house through the carriage window. "It's not that I didn't suspect something was amiss."

"That's not how I remember it," said Crispin sourly. "As I recall, Rhianna was the only person as convinced as I was that something was wrong. She said she would have come with me, if it weren't for James, and I believe she would have."

"I believe you would be right." Thayne added, "Cris, I would have come if you had only told me you were leaving."

"Well, I had no time to waste," he said dismissively.

Thayne nodded. "Yes. I agree with you there. Where is Lady Audra?"

Thayne's tone of alarm did not go unnoticed, and Crispin answered him pointedly. "I've been expecting her out of the house any moment. She's late, actually."

The sun was beginning to rise over foggy London, and Crispin had given instructions that he would take her away before dawn.

"And then what? You were just going to drive her back to Thornton alone?" asked Thayne.

Crispin shrugged. "I didn't have much of a choice."

Thayne waved his hand in the air, as if it was of no matter at this point. "I have a very disturbing letter," said Thayne, reaching into his black jacket.

"From Lady Sutherland?" asked Crispin.

"From *Lord* Sutherland," Thayne explained. "It seems Lady Sutherland is desirous of marrying Lady Audra off to her stepson."

A sudden surge of fire burned in Crispin's breast as Thayne produced the letter, and handing it over to him, Thayne said, "When Mother received little in the way of information from Lady Sutherland's letters, I took it upon myself to write directly to her husband. I played the part of ignorance, thanking him for sparing Lady Sutherland and asking if he had heard news from her. This is Lord Sutherland's response. See for yourself."

Crispin wasted no time, but unfolded the page and read:

Dear Lord Brighton,

My wife was only too happy to escort your lovely neighbor to London for the Season. She writes me daily, and I have heard nothing but wonderful things about Lady Audra. How fortunate that she has such a significant inheritance! It is our hope that she will take Stanley off our hands. A stepson from my second wife, Stanley has nothing, you see, and we would not at all mind having the house free of children. I think he is also anxious to move out, as he and my wife have not gotten on very well together. I thank you for thinking of Angela for such a charge. I hope to receive good news from them soon.

Sincerely,

Lord Sutherland

"Why did you not tell me you wrote to Lord Sutherland?" Crispin asked.

"I didn't want you to know I was as concerned as I was, only to alarm you further. I thought if I could just get some information—"

"She writes him *daily*?" Crispin cut him off, with disgust, and at once disinterested in Thayne's answer to his previous question. "All while we receive just two paltry letters…*And just who the hell is Stanley*?"

Thayne placed a calming hand on Crispin's shoulder. "I did some digging. Lord Sutherland's first wife was named Mary Everton, formerly married to a Mr. Arthur Everton. Both are deceased, but they had two sons."

Crispin went stiff at the name. "She made friends with a Lord Everton and he proposed to her. Took a while before she finally told me the name of the gent…"

"Well, she may *think* she knows a Lord Everton. If it is, indeed, Stanley Everton, then he is the penniless second son whose current permanent residence is with Lord and Lady Sutherland, known there by his proper address of *Mr.* Everton." He drew a breath and mocked, "I'm assuming she said no to him."

"Good God, Thayne." Crispin's brows pulled together and he looked out over the silent townhouse. "What time is it?"

"I believe it is time to take Lady Audra home."

• • •

Crispin pounded on the door of the Craigleath townhouse, Lord Sutherland's letter in hand and his brother Thayne standing resolutely behind him. An anxious twitch traveled down his left leg, and he tapped his foot repeatedly until the doorman appeared. Crispin stormed past the man, who only a few hours before had taken possession of the bag of clothes and promised to give them to Molly. Thayne followed closely behind him.

The lit drawing room drew their attention, and from the threshold, Crispin's gaze swept over the room. Audra was not there.

Lady Sutherland, however, was. She sat silent in her seat near the fireplace, her expression blank as Crispin stood brooding in the entrance hall.

"Lord Brighton, Lord Crispin," she said at last. "What a surprise. It's so early."

There was something in her tone that suggested their presence was of no real surprise to her at all.

Crispin stepped forward. "Where is she?" His demanding inflection alone shook the wall fixtures, while his voice resonated in the small room.

"My word, what a greeting—"

"*Where is she?*"

Cautiously, the lady rose from her seat and squared her round shoulders as best she could. She pressed her arms flat at her sides, visibly pulling folds of her skirt fabric up into balled fists.

"Sleeping, I'm sure—And just where are you going?"

She took one step forward, but Thayne gestured for her to halt, and Crispin made his way upstairs to the bedrooms.

• • •

Using the narrow stair railing and the opposite wall, Crispin propelled himself forward to the first floor. Crispin knocked at each bedroom, calling Audra's name repeatedly before entering, unconcerned with awakening either the servants or the neighbors.

At the third door, he knocked briskly, swung the door open, and found a servant girl sitting in her nightclothes at the end of the bed, her knees buckled under her chin and her arms wrapped around her legs. Crispin quickly apologized and went to close the door.

"Wait," she said, swinging her legs over the side of the bed and throwing her robe about her. "What is your name?"

Embarrassed, he begged her forgiveness and continued to leave.

"Please," she said. "Are you…" She looked behind him into the hallway and lowered her voice. "Are you Lord Crispin?"

He stopped and looked curiously at the figure that now stood beside the bed, a dark silhouette against the dawning light of the window. "I am."

"Please, don't leave," she said, her arm outstretched pleadingly. Her soft voice cut through the still air. "My name is Molly. I know why you are here. And I'm so glad of it."

Crispin heard Audra speak her name aloud in his ears. *Give the clothes to Molly.*

"What can you tell me?" he asked urgently.

"This was her room," she said, approaching him swiftly and looking farther down the hall, "but you won't find her here."

Crispin put his hand on her arm, and she turned back to face him. "Where is she? Bring me to her." Even in the dim light,

Molly was white with fear. "Bring me to Audra, and you shall always have a position in my home."

Molly breathed quickly through parted lips. "I cannot bring you to Lady Audra. She is not here," she said, "but what I have to tell you should lead you in her direction. Lord Crispin, I ask your permission to close the door."

Crispin agreed, and she turned the lock quietly behind them.

Seeing for the first time that the room containing Audra's things did not contain Audra, he pounded his fist into the wall. Turning his gaze on Molly, he urged, "Please, speak quickly."

Hastily, she told him of all that had happened, from the moment Audra donned Crispin's clothes to the arrival of unexpected visitors. All was told as she had heard it from the top of the staircase, and had occurred not two hours before.

"Lord Everton and the other man kidnapped her!" she finished, and drew what might have been the first breath she'd taken since the beginning of her story.

"To what end?" he cried.

"After they left," she told him, "I heard William, the butler, approach Lady Sutherland. He offered her his congratulations, and she said it was all thanks to him for telling her of the bag of men's clothes."

"But you said you received the clothes, and that Audra was wearing them."

"Aye, but I received them from William. He must have examined the bag's contents before giving it over to me." She added, "I am sure Lady Sutherland will recommend you release me from my duties."

"You needn't worry about that," he assured her. "Molly, is there anything else you can tell me?"

"Yes. Lady Sutherland and William began to celebrate in the drawing room with a few drinks. I continued to listen to their conversation, even as they began to slur their words, and that's when I heard them say where they were taking Audra."

"Where!" he cried.

Molly shook her head, worry for her mistress exuding from her every pore. "Gretna Green."

Chapter Ten

When Audra awoke, her head throbbed and her mouth and nose felt dry. Pounding horses' hooves, rattling carriage wheels, and the occasional cracking of a whip were harsh sounds that echoed and caused her ears to pulsate. Aware she was traveling in a carriage, she considered her position. Though her feet rested on the floor of the carriage, she was conscious that her torso lay on the leather bench, her right arm numb beneath her.

The lights that poured into the carriage cabin seemed bright, though she knew from the gray hue it was only the sensitivity of her eyes that made it seem so. The curtains were mostly drawn over the windows, but between them the sky looked charcoal gray, and the day gave the appearance of being later than it no doubt was. Audra felt as if she had had too much wine, though she knew she had not had any, and sensed she might throw up. Pushing up from the leather seat, each bump seeming excessively violent, Audra rubbed her arm and turned to her travel partner.

Lord Everton sat across from her, his expression sullen, his chocolate-brown eyes flickering from her, to his hands, then back to her again. He looked tired and stressed and—something else. A curious shadow draped Lord Everton's face. Was it guilt? She certainly hoped so. Despite having little understanding of what was happening, Audra strongly suspected any such feeling was justified.

"How are you feeling?" she heard him ask.

His voice was distant. Audra pushed back the curtain nearest her and looked out the window. The city of London was gone, replaced by a vast stretch of country, its hills and its valleys doubled in her vision.

"Where are we going?" she managed.

She felt Lord Everton follow her gaze out the window. "North."

His answer was cold, abrupt, and prompted her to turn her eyes to him. They felt sore in their sockets. She turned her head and it ached. Audra propped her tingling shoulder against the side of the cabin to support a sitting position.

"North?" she repeated, as if it were the most absurd word anyone had ever spoken. "And what am I to make of that?" When he offered nothing further, she asked with baseless hope, "Thornton?"

His eyes fell again to the clasped hands that rested in his lap. "No."

No.

The word echoed in her mind. Of course, no. Not Thornton. Never Thornton.

Raising her hands to her eyes, she rubbed, less to ease the blurred vision than to remember. What was the last thing she could recall? The details were all so unclear. She went as far back in her mind as dressing with Molly, and even then, whole scenes were cut from her memory. A vision of Lady Sutherland in the drawing room struck her and—what had they talked about? Words escaped her, but the lady's countenance stood out. She was not the silly, giddy Lady Sutherland Audra had lived with these last weeks. She was serious, severe, and cold. It was as if a veil had been dropped, and the façade that had been Lady Sutherland fluttered away. Audra could not help wondering, was no one who they seemed?

Out of her musings, one thing was as clear as water.

"Secret Admirer," she said, and the words seemed to bounce back at her from the leather squabs with fear-renewing power.

Audra recalled him standing behind her when the rag was placed over her mouth. It was the last memory she had before waking up in the carriage.

Lord Everton ran his fingers through his hair. "Mr. Thackeray," he said. His voice was quiet, calm. "Yes, I…I'm quite sorry about that."

"Secret Admirer has a *name*?" she retorted. "*You know his name?*"

"Your secret admirer," he clarified, "is an uncle of mine on my mother's side. My deceased mother. I'm sure the details are of no interest to you at this point in time."

"Your *uncle*?" she cried, her voice rasping.

"Yes."

Her mouth fell open to speak, but there were too many words, and they all fought for their chance to come out. Audra had to line them up before she could allow any to take flight.

"Lady Audra," he hurried, extending an arm out to her but retracting it suddenly, "I can assure you there is no need to fear him. He was not pursuing you." With a sharp breath, he blurted, "He was only doing what I asked. Playing a character, if you will."

Audra went still as a bitter chill bled from her heart through her veins, making her go cold from her core to her every extremity. Was this the same Lord Everton that she had known and befriended? The same Lord Everton she had confided in and leaned upon during some of her darkest hours?

"What…you…*asked*?"

"Please do not look at me so," he begged. "I know! Obviously, I owe you an explanation, Lady Audra."

I should say so, she thought, but the words did not escape her lips. She shook her head, recoiling from this person whom she clearly did not know.

"Allow me to explain my actions," he added.

She held up a hand to him. "Do not say another word to me, sir. I demand you turn this carriage around and take me back to London."

He sighed, and his shoulders slumped. "I'm afraid I simply cannot do that."

•••

Crispin's long-estranged aunt sat in the drawing room, pouring herself a cup of tea. Thayne, too, sat across from her with a calm air of courtesy in his manner that struck Crispin as sharply out of place, like a detective ready to break bread with a known, if not yet apprehended, criminal. It was not the scene of an interrogation; rather, they looked as if they were about to have a casual conversation. Indeed, they *were* having a conversation, and Crispin stood stunned in the doorframe.

"My dear nephew…"

"It's Lord Brighton to you, madam. And I believe you have some explaining to do."

Her entire person held the mien of innocence. "Whatever do you mean?"

Despite the visual, Thayne was thankfully to the point. "Have you been keeping Lady Audra in London against her will?"

Lady Sutherland pressed her hand to her buxom chest and said, "Why, goodness, what a suggestion!"

Either his brother was a fool, or had more self-control than Crispin cared to have, but it didn't matter. He had no interest in knowing his brother's meaning by attempting a dignified meeting. This was no time for dialogue, no time for discussion.

Crispin took long, leaping strides in Lady Sutherland's direction. Standing over her, he asked venomously, "*Where is she?*"

Lady Sutherland had settled herself into the large, yellow chair near the fireplace, a full cup of tea now in hand. "You are being incredibly rude, nephew, and I refuse to have a conversation with you as long as you are screaming at me."

Enraged to the point of irrational action, Crispin knocked the tea out of her hand to the floor, leaving a trail of tea in its wake from her skirt to the arm of the chair to the carpet. Thayne leapt to his feet, and with one swift movement Crispin was relocated to his brother's side, a firm hand pressed against his chest. The lady sat stunned.

"I know for a fact Lord Everton and another man took her away from here not two hours ago," Crispin declared over his brother's shoulder.

Thayne, hearing this piece of information for the first time, did not trouble to question his brother regarding the source, but turned abruptly to Lady Sutherland.

"Is this true?" Thayne asked her.

Lady Sutherland hesitated, then sprang suddenly from her chair with a slap intended for Crispin, but inadvertently stuck Thayne instead. Aside from the surprise of this, Thayne was little affected, but Lady Sutherland seemed very much so, as shown by her sudden screams for help.

Crispin leapt forward to stifle her and pressed one large hand over her mouth, the other behind her head. "Not. Another. *Sound.*"

Thayne allowed this second physical intrusion and stood over Lady Sutherland as Crispin eased her back into her yellow chair. Crispin burned a heated glare into her eyes until she shut her lids. He wanted to crush her head between his hands, and he allowed his fingers to tighten to ensure she knew it. At the same time, he recognized the need to maintain control over his anger.

"Lady Sutherland." Crispin spoke very slowly and deliberately. "You must speak with us. I will remove my hands, but you cannot scream."

Lady Sutherland breathed heavily through red nostrils. They expanded widely and contracted quickly. She opened her eyes and nodded.

Crispin released her, but Lady Sutherland was not quick to speak. She looked from Crispin to Thayne, and from Thayne to Crispin, her red face a striking contrast to the white lines that remained from where Crispin's fingers had been.

"I will not ask you again," Crispin told her, his hands curled into fists at his sides, his chest heaving from the struggle for restraint.

Thayne rested a firm, supportive hand on Crispin's forearm and turned to the lady. "Where is Lady Audra?"

"She went upstairs," Lady Sutherland said, "after the masquerade last night. It was the last I saw of her."

"It is a lie!" Crispin exclaimed, and Thayne grabbed him from behind as he lunged for her a second time. Lady Sutherland jumped backwards in her seat, and the chair fell back to the floor, and she with it.

Crispin's anger escaped in the form of a growl, and he stormed toward the opposite end of the room to regain a measure of level-headedness. Meanwhile, Thayne assisted Lady Sutherland, naught but a pile of rich velvet, to her feet.

To Crispin's surprise, she did not scream a second time. She did not cry.

She laughed.

"You never considered she might have changed her mind and run off?" she asked Crispin. "That perhaps marrying you was something to think more thoroughly about?"

"The letter, Cris."

Crispin pulled Lord Sutherland's note from his pocket and read the beginning lines:

My wife was only too happy to escort your lovely neighbor to London for the Season. She writes me daily, and I have heard nothing but wonderful things about Lady Audra. How fortunate that she has such a significant inheritance…

Lady Sutherland glared at Crispin, then Thayne. Crispin wondered what she would do now that she was caught. He was not surprised when she took on the character she had portrayed upon her arrival at Ravensleigh.

"It is hot in here, is it not?" she asked lightly.

With this, Lady Sutherland's head swayed to and fro, her eyes glazed over, and she fell limp in Thayne's arms.

• • •

"Stop the carriage!" Audra cried from the carriage window. "Driver, stop this instant!" Her words went unheeded, and she cried again, "Please, stop!"

She turned back to Lord Everton and eyed him as he sat calmly in his seat, making no motion to prevent her distressed calls.

"Why does he not stop?" she demanded.

"He will not stop," he said.

Was it his expression or his tone that gave Lord Everton an apologetic air? She hardly had energy to interpret it, but even his posture and his language gave the impression of remorse.

"I did not want it to come…to *this*," he added.

"Who is it that drives this carriage?" Audra asked.

"My uncle," he told her. "Mr. Thackeray."

With the knowledge that Secret Admirer was in control of the vehicle, Audra lowered herself back to a sitting position beside the window. Her eyes fell with her hopes as she realized the severity of her situation. And yet, despite the events in the townhouse and the fear she had felt in the presence of Lady Sutherland and Secret Admirer, she found it impossible to be fearful in the cabin with Lord Everton. At most, the oddity of the circumstances left her bewildered and increasingly angry.

"Am I to take it that you are kidnapping me, Lord Everton?"

He pressed his fist to his lips and exhaled forcefully through his nostrils. "There is so much to tell you."

"You were my *friend*. I trusted you."

"You can trust me still," he told her. "If only you would let me account for this decidedly bizarre affair…"

"Very well, Lord Everton," she said, her sharp tongue cutting off his last words. "Seeing as how we will be together in this carriage until you determine it is time to stop, enlighten me with your tale."

She was hardly conscious that she was glaring at him from across the carriage, her shoulders squared, her chin lifted defiantly, and her hands clasped tightly in her lap. She only wondered briefly if this was how her governess, Mauvreen, felt when expecting an explanation from her often gentle but occasionally disobedient student.

Lord Everton leaned forward, his elbows resting on his knees and his fingers intertwined loosely in what Audra suspected was a move calculated to give the appearance of casualness, but a twitch in his left eye and a gleam of sweat at his brow told her otherwise.

"I will begin my tale in the hope that you will, after a time, become more receptive to my words," he said, his fingers flexing, each pressing against the tips of the matching finger opposite, and then combing together again. After a long pause, and not a few deep breaths, he said, "Initially, it was my hope that you would find the love letters from your secret admirer flattering. I...I drafted them myself, hoping with each one to steal a piece of your heart away from Lord Crispin."

His words floated in the air between them until they dropped on Audra one at a time, in no particular order, until the whole lot of them sat in a heap. She felt herself struggling to organize them, to make sense of them, and when at last they were all sorted out, she viewed them in their tidy arrangement with only one question forming in her mind.

"You wrote...?" she whispered.

She felt her lips quiver, but she was unsure whether this meant she was enraged, about to burst into tears, or something else entirely. Audra was numb from head to toe, and listened on.

"I hoped even further," he said, ignoring her words, "that you would become enamored with the idea of a secret admirer and, gradually, with the secret admirer himself, despite his undisclosed identity." He paused, but if he expected a response, Audra was in no position to speak to him again. At last he continued, "I hoped to reveal myself as this secret admirer and confess my devotion to you. It was my plan to gain your affection." He ran his fingers through his almond-brown hair and closed his hands over the lower half of his face. "Obviously, that did not work," he added, in a way that made it seem improvised and not part of his original script. "Once it became clear to me that my letters were, in fact, distressing you, my plan changed. My uncle, Mr. Thackeray, acted as your obsessive secret admirer only to deflect suspicion from me. When you began to confide your concerns to me—well, my hopes were lifted. I became determined to show you a display of my devotion to you and your safety. So I plotted the dramatic scene at the Meryton's, from your frightening encounter with Secret Admirer to my chasing him out the window and down the balcony. After all, I thought, how could you not fall in love with the hero who saved you from the clutches of evil Secret Admirer?"

He's insane, she thought. *Good Lord, all this time, Lord Everton was insane, and I did not know it.*

"Did your uncle murder Lord Garrington?" she asked pointedly, recalling the jewelry box his mistress had found beside his body.

"I admit," he told her cautiously, "my uncle is not the finest of company. Murder, however, was never a part of the plan."

"What does that mean?"

"Lady Audra, it is not my way to ask questions I have no business asking. I know Lord Garrington was an acquaintance of my uncle from years past. If my uncle felt threatened by the lord's knowledge of certain events…if he murdered Lord Garrington, he acted on his own. I have every intention of limiting my association with him once we are settled."

Settled? Audra felt quite disgusted, and she clamped her jaw to avoid speaking without thought.

"After the 'rescue,'" Lord Everton continued, "when you did not fall into my arms with the appreciation of a lover, but treated me no differently than as if your father had come to your aid…"

He stopped. The memory seemed to overtake him, and his face twisted with a tormented look. Audra wondered if the original event had been as painful, or if this display was the result of considerable time spent in the misery of reflection.

"Well," he said, taking a turn in the commentary, "giving up was out of the question. The future that I saw—that I see—for us is too great to relinquish. I thought perhaps I had put too much store in flirtations and casual interactions. I came to realize that even a single act of heroism is not enough to win a lady's affections. She must have something certain to lay her heart against. I thought myself ridiculous for not seeing it before. A proposal of marriage was naturally the next step."

Audra thought back to the morning of his proposal and sat amazed that he had taken her rejection so well. At the time, it was Lady Sutherland who had reacted outrageously. Lord Everton swiftly continued with his story, allowing her no time to explore the memory in any depth.

"I wanted this to be *your* decision. When you rejected my hand, I don't know how I bore it, except to suppose that you needed more time. Time I would have gladly given you, if there had been time left to give. But there was the murder investigation I needed to distance myself from. And then you made your plans to leave London…with *him*…"

"How did you—?"

"…and I had no choice but to fall back on my last resort."

Audra considered possible scenarios where Lord Everton might have learned of her plans with Crispin, made only hours earlier. Audra was certain her conversation with Crispin at the masquerade had not been overheard. And yet, somehow he knew. Somehow, their secret was found out.

"And do you expect to make me fall in love with you by kidnapping me?" she asked.

Lord Everton shifted in his seat. He examined his palms, opening and closing them in his lap.

Suddenly, he turned his eyes upon her, and a soft expression followed. "Please believe me when I say that I do care for you, Lady Audra. Audra." He stopped and rolled his tongue over his lips, as if the spoken name left a sugary sweetness upon them. "I truly love you. I hope one day you will love me in return."

Audra turned her head to look out the window of the speeding carriage, a waft of Crispin's scent escaping the jacket and filling her senses with a sensation of calm and courage.

"I shall never see you again after today," she told him.

Lord Everton met her coolness with an icy statement of his own. "I think you shall see a great deal of me after we are married."

Married? Audra turned a piercing gaze at him, and speaking through the fire that rose from her core, she asked, "I beg your pardon, sir?"

"You must understand," he went on, "I could no longer leave the decision in your hands. I make you this promise—that I will take excellent care of you. In time, I have no doubt you will see the value of a husband who cherishes you above all things, and indeed learn to love me in return."

"You cannot be serious," she managed.

"I assure you, I am very serious." He settled himself in his seat and loosened his tie. "You should make yourself comfortable, Lady Audra. It is over three hundred miles from London to Gretna Green. You are in for a long ride."

Chapter Eleven

Crispin and Thayne solicited the assistance of Lords Whitehall and Meryton, and the gentlemen wasted no time in making their way to Queen Anne Street. There, they were briefed on the delicacy and seriousness of the situation and commissioned to remain at Lady Sutherland's side should she attempt to escape. She had come out of her feigned faint, and was sitting very gravely in the yellow chair by the fireplace with the air of an undomesticated animal whose next move is wildly uncertain.

Meanwhile, a search for William revealed the butler had collected his things and left of his own accord some time after Crispin and Thayne's arrival, but with sufficient information from Molly they prepared to chase after Everton. Only a final interview with Lady Sutherland stood in their way.

Crispin was too emotional and far too anxious to be on their way to attempt any further communication with Lady Sutherland. He watched from the drawing room doorway as his brother knelt beside the lady and approached her calmly and kindly.

"Lady Sutherland," Thayne addressed, "we already know Mr. Everton is leading Lady Audra to Gretna Green. I am sure you also realize Crispin and I will follow after them momentarily. I appeal to you, upon everything that is good, knowing the fine qualities that exist in our mother must also exist in you, to tell us anything at all that will assist in bringing this doomed scheme to a swifter end."

The lady refused to meet his gaze and remained silent, though from the tilt of her head in Thayne's direction, Crispin was sure she was listening.

Thayne continued, "For example, the name of an inn? How far they anticipated traveling today? Where they hoped to change horses?" He gave her a moment, and when she refused to grace him with a reply, he added, "Assist us, and we shall see to it your punishment is lessened."

At this last, she turned and sneered at him. "You and I both know this scandalous affair must remain quiet to maintain Lady Audra's reputation. Bring me up on charges of kidnapping, and she will be ruined."

Crispin watched his brother closely, and marveled. His patience was saintly, and she roused no physical stir from him with her words. Thayne satisfied himself with a verbal warning.

"I would advise you not to presume what action we will take, Lady Sutherland. I offer you one final opportunity. What can you tell us about Lady Audra's whereabouts?"

The lady clamped her jaw, and Thayne acknowledged the implication of her response by arising from his kneeling position.

Addressing Lords Whitehall and Meryton, Thayne instructed, "See to it she does not leave this house until you hear word from us."

The gentlemen were preparing to make themselves comfortable when Lady Sutherland suddenly blurted, "It seems ridiculous to say they took the Great North Road, as that's all anyone would ever take to Scotland." Thayne turned to meet her gaze, and she added crossly, "They hoped the horses would make it as far as Stevenage."

"Thank you," Thayne responded. Turning to the lords, he said hurriedly, "See to it that Lady Sutherland collects her things and is on her way back to the country today."

They nodded. As to the search for Audra, Lord Meryton's curricle with its two swift horses was offered to the cause, and Crispin and Thayne departed in it to give chase.

• • •

Several hours passed, and like the road they traveled, time stretched long. The curricle was swift, and the horses seemed as ready to give chase as the men they carried, but the brothers spoke little as the miles passed away beneath them. Stress weighed heavy in the air. Armed with naught but the name of Stanley Everton and Lady Sutherland's word they hoped to push their horses to Stevenage, the initial galvanization to action gave way to doubt. Crispin believed it unlikely that Everton would have stopped within the first ten miles of the trip, but as Great North Road extended onward, the inns and taverns along the way each became a possibility. He suddenly felt compelled to stop at each town, while his inner voice assured him that if they stopped at every town along the way they were certain never to catch up to them.

At twenty miles, the horses had grown tired. Thayne agreed they should stop in Hatfield to refresh them and make inquiries at the Eight Bells Inn. Their description of the three travelers from London—an old man with salt-and-pepper hair, a lord in his thirties, and a well-dressed, teenage boy—brought no success. The inn was filled mostly with locals, and the few travelers who had come had been singular—and none at all from London. They carried on; knowing that even at a slower pace the horses would bring them to Stevenage within two hours' time.

Crispin knew they were close when Thayne slowed the curricle. "What are you doing?"

"Look there," said Thayne, gesturing with the reins to the road before them.

Crispin squinted through an uncommonly foggy, midday horizon and nearly stood at the sight of the distant stagecoach. "You think it's them?"

Thayne pressed a heartened hand on his brother's back. "Perhaps. Let us not close in on them, but see where they turn."

Crispin nodded, and for a quarter of an hour they followed at a distance. Without the impetus of their previous pace, this span of road quickly became the longest of their journey and their environment more prominent than before. Previously, Crispin's eyes had been upon the unseen goal that lay ahead, and he knew little of what surrounded him. He had paid mind neither to the brisk wind that had continually slapped at them for some five hours, nor the varying scenes that played along Great North Road. Now, for the first time, the chilly temperature began to pinch at his face, and the country around them seemed overwhelmingly vast and ominously opposed to their success.

At last, with impassioned hearts they observed the stagecoach snake its way to High Street, Stevenage, and pause before the White Hart Inn. Thayne halted their own horses beside a tavern a few doors down. With stilled breath Crispin waited for the stagecoach passengers to alight, grateful that the midday sun had not burned off the thick fog that cloaked them from any watchful eyes.

•••

Hours of silence on Audra's part did not hinder Lord Everton's influx of promises and vows as they rode along in the carriage. Using every expression of speech, he promised Audra his complete devotion, and swore on the graves of more persons that she herself had ever been acquainted with that her happiness with him would be complete. He gave his word, of all the women he had met, there was not one of them who had so fully enraptured him, who filled his every intellectual need, and whose physical features elevated her to so flawless and exquisite a position as Audra herself. He pronounced himself convinced, out of the women he had met and the women he had yet to meet, there was none who could match her unrivaled feminine perfection, and that his life would be above all things devoted to her every wish. He declared her everything a woman ought to be, and declared himself her humble servant, provider, and protector.

More convinced than ever of his insanity, Audra remained silent until they arrived at the inn. She refused to allow the emotional turmoil within to overtake her, but demanded it remain in check. Indeed, she made a deal with her emotions, that until she could figure her way out of this, they would remain dormant. Only once she escaped would she give them their due attention, and indeed welcome them with open arms. It was an agreeable arrangement to all.

Thus, she spent the hours of travel deep in thought. She schemed and calculated scenarios and conjured possibilities to make her flight. She was very glad to be still in Crispin's clothing, and she tucked the occasional rogue curl back up under her hat. Her first priority upon entering the inn was to keep her identity as a female secret. This was critical, and must be carried out with no amount of carelessness. That she remained a boy to the patrons of the inn was crucial to avoiding the disastrous happenstance of being compromised and thus forced to marry Lord Everton.

When the stagecoach came to a stop, Secret Admirer—Mr. Thackeray—opened the door for her. She retracted.

"Never fear, my love," said Lord Everton. "He means you no harm."

Audra clamped down her jaw, stood, and refused Mr. Thackeray's assistance down from the carriage. After all, a boy would not accept the hand of another man, would he?

Then, with Lord Everton's hand upon her neck, she felt him step down behind her. She shivered more at the sensation of his stern hand than the chilly air, and glanced at the door of the White Hart Inn. The tavern was lively. Men could be heard singing drunkenly to old folk songs, and women laughed in shrill, mischievous hoots.

A sudden impulse to flee came over her, and she stole a quick glance to her left, then her right. Audra suspected she could run quickly dressed in Crispin's pants, but where to go…

Her heart stopped as the figure of a young man stood on his curricle. The fog was a dense gray that made visibility short and muddy, but there was nothing indistinct about the outlined frame she saw through the cloudy mist. That he saw her, as well, was all that prevented a scream from escaping her lips, and as Thayne stood beside him and they nonchalantly disembarked from the vehicle, she felt the fear abate with the certainty of rescue at hand.

Then, muscled between her two captors, Audra was ushered into the inn.

Mr. Thackeray quickly had a woman on each side of him, and arm-in-arm they made their way to the taproom.

"Keep your head down," Lord Everton instructed Audra.

Audra did as he instructed. She was glad not to look around. The place was rowdy and seedy for an afternoon crowd, and the atmosphere made her nervous. Audra saw the flow of a red skirt with a black lace hem greet her and Lord Everton where they stood near the threshold.

"Well," said the wearer, in a high-pitched, intoxicated voice, "look at what we have here! A couple of gentlemen come to spend the night?"

Lord Everton spoke in a monotone voice, but it held an air of command. "My brother is unwell, and I would like a room for him to rest in while our horses are changed. If you can spare one, we would be much obliged."

"How much obliged?" she asked, swinging her red skirt to and fro and drawing riotous laughter from a few of the male patrons.

"A room, if you please," he said.

"A drink first, perhaps? We've got beer, gin, rum…"

"Just a room."

Audra cast a flickering glance through her lashes to view her—a round-faced girl, with brown, wispy hair, a large bosom, not more than twenty.

Smiling, the girl nodded assent. "Betsy, won't you show these boys upstairs?" Addressing Audra, she said, "Feel better, aye?"

Lord Everton must have nodded or given some other gesture of acknowledgment, and she left them to the care of the one named Betsy.

"This way," Betsy said.

Up a set of creaking, wooden steps, Betsy led them down a hallway of doors. Behind each one, there seemed just as many boisterous noises as in the taproom downstairs. Glass frequently smashed about, laughter filled the air, and not a few wanton grunts and groans bounced along the airy hallway, with no curtains or carpet to absorb the sounds.

"Here you are," Betsy said, opening a door to an empty room for them.

Audra felt a nudge from Lord Everton as they crossed the threshold. A moment later, the door was closed behind them.

• • •

Lord Everton kicked off his shoes carelessly and sat upon the bed. Audra casually made her way to the nearest window and, half-seated upon the sill, stole a glance through the glass. Even through the thick grayness she could see nothing to support an effort to climb down—no clematis, no nearby tree, nothing but a straight drop between the White Hart and the next building over. Jumping was a possibility, but not one she liked to entertain.

Without knowing either Crispin and Thayne's whereabouts, or Lord Everton's intensions, Audra bided her time. For the first time in several hours, she spoke.

"Lord Everton, why do you not get us something to drink?"

He removed his hat and gestured it toward a center table. "There is tea. If you are thirsty, I will pour you a cup."

Audra hesitated. "I had something a bit stronger in mind." She suspected he would not leave her to retrieve drinks from the taproom, but it couldn't hurt to try.

"I want us to remember this afternoon," he told her.

At sixteen, Audra was innocent, but she understood to what he alluded, and she demanded he say it outright. "And what is it, Lord Everton, that I am to remember?"

He smiled. "You're due for a wedding night."

"It is not night. We are not married."

"*Yet*," he injected. "And really, what difference makes a day or two? Or, for that matter, the time of day? We shall be husband and wife in no time at all. I, for one, see no need for our fleshly expressions to be put off when a mere few hours by carriage remains before our nuptials. Do relax, my dear Lady Audra, and make yourself comfortable."

At this, her mind turned to thoughts of defense. She examined the room for items of possible weaponry. A pewter candleholder? An oil lamp? The last made her shiver, as she struggled with her old feelings for Lord Everton. Yes, despite everything, she still wished not to set him afire. The hours that had passed had not been enough for her to reconcile Lord Everton, her friend, with Lord Everton, her kidnapper.

Lord Everton, your violator, an internal voice said to her.

No sooner did she register them than the words helped her recognize she must be willing to use any means for escape. The room, however, proved disappointing in the way of armaments. It had only the very bare essentials, and pewter candleholders were not to be found. A plainly made bed. A pine dresser. A faded brown rug. A stubbly little candle sitting in a dish. No oil lamp.

A sudden fury took her over, and she turned to him. "And just what sort of relationship do you imagine us having?" she asked sharply. "Do you believe I could tolerate you after being taken from the man I love? After being forced to marry you against my will? After learning of your tricks and falsehoods?"

Her passion seemed not to faze him. "In time, you will see how well I treat you. I am convinced you will see the purity of my affection and recover."

She drew a sharp breath. "You, sir, do not know me at all."

Impulsively, Audra pushed herself away from the windowsill and made for the door. She dared not look behind to see his response, but she could hear the swiftness of his feet on the wooden floor. Audra turned the lock and reached for the handle, while in the same instant Lord Everton's hands landed upon her shoulders.

She had too much pride to struggle, but merely stiffened herself as he besieged her and turned her body round to face him. Seizing her in his arms, he crushed her small frame against his wider, stronger body with frightening smoothness, as if the action was as easy for him as a waltz.

Audra struggled for air. In Lord Everton's grasp, her ribs were confined in an immoveable position; her lungs left no room to expand. Her open mouth gasped for breath, and she thought she would choke to death when his tongue pressed against hers. The movement of his hot, wet mouth closing over hers brought her to panic, and she turned her head every which way, desperate for the smallest trace of oxygen. The motion seemed only to excite him, and his fingers curled around her back with suffocating restrictiveness.

Panic waved over her as she tottered on the edge of unconsciousness. Then, suddenly, Lord Everton pulled back and looked at her, releasing the tightness of his grasp. Audra's vision blurred, she felt her forehead fall to his chest, and she gasped wildly. She was hardly aware that he held her to her feet as her own legs gave way beneath her.

"Oh, darling," he said to her, "I've never had this much of an effect on a woman." His voice was distant to Audra's ears, but the unmistakable, swelling pride was sickening. "Now, surely, you see we were meant to be together."

She forced herself to inhale through her nostrils and exhale slowly through her mouth. Soon, her vision returned and her strength was restored. She lifted her head to meet his gaze.

"You stupid fool!" she exclaimed, beating his chest with her fist. "Do you mean to choke me to death?"

Lord Everton stood with a dumbfounded expression. "I…"

Then, with all the breath in her body, she shouted, "*I shall never marry you!*"

In that moment, the bedroom door was kicked inward. Lord Everton released Audra as they each fell to the floor, splinters of wood scattering around them.

The moment happened so quickly, Audra hardly knew how she came to be on the old, brown rug of the room. But through a second set of eyes, removed from her body, she watched the event unfold at the slowest of speeds. And when Thayne overtook Lord Everton, she felt a warm, familiar tug upon her hand, a loving arm about her waist, and with a gentle lift she found herself back on her feet. In that moment, only one thing mattered, and it was not that she had been imprisoned in London for weeks; it was not that Lord Everton was a liar and a fraud; it was not the bruises she knew would inevitably reveal themselves in a vast array of purples, yellows, and blues.

What mattered was that Crispin was at her side.

• • •

Thayne's well-placed right hook left Lord Everton groggy in the corner chair he had fallen into. His shirt was ripped, his collar ruffled, and his head was propped up by one hand that appeared ready to give way at any moment. Sweat poured down from his brow, and he shut his eyes as he appeared to recall the possibilities that had crashed to pieces around him.

"We could have had such a life together," he lamented to Audra, turning his gaze to her. "I was going to take care of you. I was going to be your everything. I was going to…"

"You were going to allow her fortune to make you a very wealthy man, is that not right, Mr. Everton?" Thayne interjected.

"Mister?" Audra repeated. She turned to her beloved for clarification. "Crispin?"

"It's true," Crispin told her, holding her in his arms as if she were as delicate as a porcelain vase. "Lord Everton is no lord at all."

"He is Mr. Stanley Everton," Thayne added, "the adopted second son of Lord Sutherland by way of his deceased wife, formerly known as Miss Mary Everton. He has no inheritance whatsoever, and his stepmother—that is, Lady Sutherland—has been anxious to get him out of the house."

Audra felt ill. "So that is the connection to Lady Sutherland, is it?" she asked at last. "It was she who hoped for this connection and thought keeping me in London would change my feelings from Crispin to her stepson?" She paused, the revelation cutting her faith in her own species. "And when I did not," she finally managed, "Lady Sutherland allowed…agreed…to *this*?"

With her hand in Crispin's, she took a few steps toward the man called Mr. Everton, her brows furrowed.

Addressing him, she asked, "What have you to say for yourself, Lord Everton?"

"Mister," Crispin corrected.

Mr. Everton made no reply except to slump low into his chair and twitch his fingers across his face.

"Oh! This is insanity!" cried Audra. Her entire body shook with outrage. "You fooled me! You singled me out, pursued my friendship, acted as my confidant and protector, while secretly intending to have me for yourself no matter what the cost?" She scolded, "Shame on you, Mr. Everton. Shame on you and your family. To think you were one of the only people I ever looked forward to seeing, you who were always kind and gentlemanly— and all along it was because of you that I was unable to go home. Did I not I make it very clear in no uncertain terms that I was dedicated to Crispin? Dishonorable man! I am mortified by my very acquaintance with you. You are the very embodiment of repugnance, and I wish you a humiliation and shame so widespread that no woman can be taken by your performances ever again."

Her words had their effect. Mr. Stanley Everton rose from his chair, opened the window behind him, and leapt to the building below.

Chapter Twelve

April 30, 1836—London

Lady Sutherland, like her stepson, returned to the country in disgrace. Reports of the lady's campaign to marry Audra to her penniless stepson quickly became popular conversation in the assembly halls. As the even worse rumors that she had kept Audra in London against her will for just such a purpose filled the ears of the aristocracy, Lady Sutherland's reputation fell swiftly into shambles. All members of the Brighton and Kingsley families found comfort that neither she nor Mr. Everton, whose name was also connected with the alleged affair, would be able to show themselves in public again. Rumors that Mr. Everton had fled to Scotland soon followed.

Further evidence from the murder of Lord Garrington led the authorities to narrow their list of suspects down to one. Mr. Thackeray, as told by Lords Whitehall and Meryton, had integrated himself into good society under the assumed name of Lord Smyth. Alas, they would never have the opportunity of trying him for the murder. In fact, Mr. Thackeray never left the White Hart Inn the day of Audra's kidnapping. A fight in the taproom left him with a knife wound of his own—one that he would not recover from.

Audra was as anxious as ever to return home, but the one, final delay that kept her in London for yet another two weeks was a welcomed one. St. George's in Hanover Square was a very fashionable place to be married, and Crispin's suggestion of obtaining a special license did not meet with any great reluctance from his bride. After all, it was not so much Thornton itself that she wished to return to as the beloved people who resided there. Now, all had come to London for an April thirtieth wedding. The London townhouse on Queen Anne Street was instantly transformed as it filled with people whom Audra loved. Indeed, its atmosphere was almost as cozy and familiar as being back in the country, save for one thing.

Lady Moira Brighton was especially horrified at her sister's actions toward Audra, and took a great deal of blame upon herself for the events that had taken place. Indeed, it seemed that no amount of assurances from Audra, Rhianna, or her sons could convince her she had no way of knowing her sister's intentions. In the end, it was Audra's father, Guilford, Lord Kingsley, who at last eased her troubled mind and assured her that, unpleasant a situation though it was, there was certainly no blame to be placed upon her and there was nothing that could affect the ties between both Kingsleys and Brightons.

Thus, Lady Brighton, Rhianna Brighton, Miss Mauvreen, and Molly surrounded Audra as she dressed in her Presentation Day gown that cherished April morning, replacing her headdress of three feathers with a wreath of pink flower blossoms and a veil of Honiton lace. Her bare arms, as had been required by court, were now covered with a fine silk shawl to shield her from the spring morning chill and to hide the unsightly purples, yellows, and blues that had appeared on her fair skin following the scene at the White Hart Inn. Lady Brighton offered her daughter-in-law the diamond necklace she had worn the day of her wedding to Crispin's father, and Audra wore it proudly, along with a pearl and diamond brooch from Rhianna.

On the west side of the church, St. George's six Corinthian columns awaited her. At their center a long, velvet rug ran from the altar inside the church out the front door, along the portico, and down the stone steps to the street. Audra exited the carriage with her eyes on the double wooden doors just beyond that would lead her directly to Crispin and to the life she so desperately awaited, especially these last few weeks.

Inside St. George's, Audra saw little of the heavy canopy over the pulpit, the massive painting of the Last Supper painted by William Kent above the altar, or the double-decker reading desk beside it. Neither could she focus on the small audience that included not only Brightons, but Whitehalls and Merytons. As her father, Lord Kingsley, led her down the aisle, her vision was focused on but one subject, and that one subject was equally focused on her. Lord Crispin stood at the end of that velvet rug, and she could hardly wait to take her place beside him.

Her hearing, like her vision, was selective, and when the vicar opened the *Book of Common Prayer*, she heard in part:

"Dearly beloved, we are gathered here in the sight of God, and in the face of this congregation, to join together this man and this woman in holy matrimony…"

It was a long ceremony, and Audra recognized halfway through that it was, indeed, *very* long. After their vows were repeated, she began to search the Vicar for some sign that it would soon end and, seeing none, decided it best to return to her previous state of incoherency. The pupils of Crispin's eyes were a window to their future life, and she watched scenes play out in blissful daydreams as the vicar went on with his reading.

"Let us pray…Send thy blessing upon these thy servants…so these persons may surely perform and keep the vow and covenant betwixt them made…and may ever remain in perfect love and peace together, and live according to thy laws; through Jesus Christ our Lord. Amen."

Audra started as the vicar took her right hand, and placing it together with Crispin's, added, "Those whom God hath joined together let no man put asunder."

She turned excitedly to Crispin as the vicar said, "Forasmuch as Crispin Brighton and Audra Kingsley have consented together in holy wedlock, and have witnessed the same before God and this company…I pronounce that they be man and wife together. Amen."

"At long last!" said Crispin, smiling.

"Oh! It is done," said Audra, with tears.

And with a look of deep disapproval, the vicar continued with the quite unfinished ceremony. Only it was not as long now to Audra, and she suspected it was not so long to Crispin, for the important part was done—they were husband and wife. And despite another blessing, two further readings from Psalms, the Lord's Prayer, more prayers, and a final declaration of the duties of both husband and wife, there was not a word of it that could displease her.

...

Four white horses awaited the happy couple outside St. George's, and soon the wedding chariot transported the newly joined husband and wife to the Whitehalls', where a wedding breakfast in honor of Lord Crispin and Lady Audra Brighton was held.

The hearty congratulations of friends and family were offered over stewed oysters, mayonnaise of fowl, cold game, and a ten-course, fanciful feast that included rabbit, roast mutton, and apple tarts on dishes garnished with rose petals and white doilies. English teas, bubbling champagnes, strawberries with clotted cream, and a considerable amount of fruitcake covered in orange blossoms contributed to the happiness of all. The music of violins and harps, the dancing of waltzes and reels only added to the joyous atmosphere.

The time at last came for the happy couple to depart for their honeymoon at the Kingsley's Irish estate, Wyndgate. Audra changed into her traveling clothes and bonnet—the latter of which she intended to remove the moment they were out of view.

After much hugging and kissing of beloved friends and family goodbye, Audra wrapped her hand tightly around Crispin's arm as they walked toward their carriage.

"Are you quite ready to leave London, my dear Lady Audra Brighton?" asked Crispin with a twinkle in his eye.

Placing her other hand upon his arm and pulling him close, she declared, "Ireland is not far enough!"

More From This Author
from Crimson Romance

(From *Rhianna*)

Manoir Vallière, France, 1832

Ordinarily, it would have been a predictable morning at the estate. The autumn air was crisp and the sky cloudless as the girls and their horses enjoyed an early trot along the property's meadows and grassland. Neither could have had any knowledge of the peculiar guest who was shortly to arrive at the *manoir*, nor of the events that his visit would inspire.

On this morning, Rhianna Braden reflected on her life as she rode through the fields alongside her companion, Soleil Vallière. Perhaps it was the want of conversation between them that led to this rapt musing, though such thoughts had been a frequent pastime as of late. Still, she was surprised when a vivid girlhood memory came suddenly upon her.

"They mean to send me away!" she heard her young voice exclaim.

It was now ten years since she had been sent to Madame Chandelle's School for Girls at the tender age of nine, but she recalled her cries as clearly as when she first spoke them.

"Who means to send you away?"

The voice was soothing, its owner affectionate. Rhianna often still thought of her—her only friend in England. The person whose acquaintance she could never admit to having, their precious few visits shrouded in secrecy. Worst of all, it was impossible to write to this person, hence, all communication had long since been cut off.

"Father and mother."

The words still stung after all these years. At the time she spoke them, her cheeks were moist and her eyes misty—Rhianna could almost feel the dampness on her skin now, before she pushed the memory away.

Of course, if she had only known then what a positive change her move to France would be, she would have spared herself the hot tears that soaked her childhood pillow. Now, skilled in all the accomplishments of young womanhood and residing in the Vallière home as one of the family, Rhianna wondered at this decade of transition from an English curate's daughter to a teacher at Madame Chandelle's to working as a companion to Soleil.

Indeed, at nineteen, her days were consumed with the Vallières and their activities. The bond that developed among them was, from the beginning, immediate and mutual—a bond Rhianna did not think possible to exist in a family. She recalled the first time her own parents had rejected a visit from her how the Vallières demonstrated their kindness by taking her into their home; Rhianna hoped always to reflect the generosity they continued to show throughout her years of acquaintance with them.

Their silence continued until the girls reached the easternmost plateau of the grounds. It was a favorite lookout place of theirs and, as on all mornings in this particular spot, a breathtaking scene lay before them. All the valleys of the neighboring properties came into view, draped in golden sunlight. Acres upon acres of flourishing, untamed land met them, accented in beaming rays of early morning light and outlined by sharply peaked mountains against the distant horizon. Never was there a more splendid place to fully immerse oneself in the deepest of contemplation, and it was here that the two girls reined in their horses.

After a moment's pause, Soleil's meditations were broken and she turned to Rhianna with an anxious look.

"What were your impressions of Count Armand Deveraux last night, Rhianna? You know how I trust your judgment and I am positively desperate for your opinion. I seem to be remarkably well aware of what my own is, but I fear my mind is clouded."

Rhianna tugged on the reins to ease her steed that, at the sight of a rabbit, had become restless. She could not suppress a smile.

"Certainly, his good qualities cannot be doubted," Rhianna observed. "From what time we spent with him—though not opportunity enough to perceive the most intimate details of his character—I managed to form a very high opinion of him. And he seemed very much to fancy you."

Soleil's dimples deepened in her cheeks. "We may have an opportunity of being in his acquaintance again in a few days' time. Will you do me the favor of paying particular attention to his disposition? I am certain to be blinded the moment I am in his presence!"

Rhianna promised to do as much, and added, "From his sweetness alone, one would imagine his person could only improve upon further acquaintance." Brushing the horse's mane with her fingers to further calm him, Rhianna concluded, "I confess, too, his appearance was very agreeable, very striking. His voice, expression, countenance—I cannot say I have before met a man whom I would deem so worthy of consideration for my dearest friend." Soleil smiled broadly, and Rhianna added, "Of course, if you were to marry, I don't know what I would do with myself!"

"Rhianna," Soleil quickly reflected, "you must know I am not the only one with such possibilities in my future. Each passing day I anticipate a confession from you." When Rhianna offered a perplexed look, Soleil more daringly questioned, "Has he not *yet* expressed his feelings?"

Rhianna was left no choice but to affirm her puzzlement. "I cannot think who you mean, Soleil."

Leaning closer, as though she might be overheard, Soleil hinted, "Someone with whom we are both most intimately acquainted."

Rhianna spoke the thoughts that came to her mind. "Surely, you cannot mean Philippe."

Her friend's sudden blush betrayed her thoughts.

"Soleil, you are quite imaginative, I declare!" Rhianna cried. "He views me in the same manner in which he views you, as his sister. There can be no deeper feelings on his account."

Soleil insisted otherwise. "On my word, Rhianna, Philippe is quite in love with you and has been, you may be assured, since the day you entered into our very house."

"I cannot believe so positively absurd a notion."

"And, pray, where is the absurdity in it? Do you find my brother so lacking in sense as to *not* fall in love with a girl so learned and handsome as the one I see before me?"

Rhianna could barely find words, as Soleil insisted her red curls and green eyes had quite done him in.

"In all seriousness, Soleil, why would a man who could have his pick of all the loveliest and wealthiest women in France ever consider the daughter of an English *curate*? It's preposterous!"

"Did you not see his expression as he danced with you last night? Mind you, it is the same expression he always has when he dances with you. You put him into quite a stupor!"

"If Philippe had any such expression, it was most certainly due to the wine," she returned, with a laugh.

Thus, Rhianna made it apparent that no persuasion, no matter how convincing, could influence her to believe that Philippe Vallière was in love with her and Soleil pursued it little further.

With these final reflections, the girls returned their attention to the landscape before making their way back toward the stables.

• • •

Had Soleil not been so excessively tired from the previous night's dance—not to mention the sleeplessness that resulted from meeting a handsome gentleman—she would have accompanied Rhianna on her walk through the garden. As it was, Soleil bid *adieu* to her companion at the stables and entered the manor house.

Rhianna, resolved to enjoy the morning air a while longer, wandered along under sapphire skies in peaceful intimacy with the nature surrounding her. Leisurely, she strolled among the flowers, breathing in their pleasant fragrances. There was evidence of perfection in every turn and Rhianna felt, as she often did, that walking through this garden was much like walking through a painting—a painting where no leaf had gone astray and no flower wanted a petal. Perhaps, she mused, the gardens of Kingsley Manor imitated a similar design…

As she twirled the leaf of a rhododendron bush between her fingers, a mental image of the house brought a smile to her face. Kingsley Manor, the great manor house that sat atop the hill beside her old English cottage, the very staple of her girlhood dreams of petticoats and pearls. She had dreams of it still.

Thus transported, Rhianna recalled a girlhood conversation with a young neighbor, Brenna:

"Just once, Brenna, I would like to walk up a Kingsley Manor staircase or to dance in its ballroom. Just once, I would like to have a necklace with matching earrings and gloves for my gown."

"That would be lovely," Brenna replied, wistfully. "And perhaps, too, some handsome fellow would ask you to dance."

When she caught sight of Philippe Vallière entering the garden from the opposite side, her reminiscences came to an end.

"Philippe." She smiled widely at the sight of him. "What brings you to the garden this morning?"

His lips curled in response. "I cannot see how it was to be avoided, on such a day."

"Well, you must have read my thoughts," she declared, as Philippe approached her. "I was only just this moment feeling the ache of having no one to share this inspiration with. The garden is so enchanting."

"Unquestionably, it is that," he asserted, his manner distracted. "There is something about it today that makes it more so than usual."

Unaware of any hidden implications, Rhianna readily agreed.

Seeming at once to forget the garden, Philippe went on, "I am glad of finding you. Indeed, I have searched for you all morning."

"Have you?"

"Yes. Rhianna, I must speak with you on a subject that has consumed me as of late."

Not his words only, but also the manner in which he spoke them caught her attention acutely. All fascination with the garden was lost as her eyes met his and she beheld in them the agitation of his emotions. Philippe appeared to be in a state so ill at ease that she was certain she had never seen him thus in their ten years' acquaintance.

"It is of the utmost importance," he added.

Rhianna recalled her earlier conversation with Soleil, but dismissed it at once, unable to conceive he was, in fact, or would ever, head toward the delicate subject of love.

"I can see that it is," she replied with care. "Philippe, I have not before seen you so distressed. Pray, do not leave me in wonder."

"You must not, Rhianna, mistake my anxiousness for distress. My affliction is one of joyful anticipation. And you alone can relieve me of my restlessness, allay me from this malady."

Rhianna was earnest in her concern. "Philippe, I have not the privilege of understanding you…"

"No, indeed, you do not, for I have been too concealing in my behavior. Repeatedly have I asked wherefore? To what end should I suppress it? For years have I kept silent, my soul restrained and inwardly anguished while awaiting the sensible and perfect moment—but no more! My secret shall be masked no longer. For my own sanity it cannot!"

His meaning could no longer be mistaken. These opening words produced a shock in Rhianna, for they were beyond everything she could have supposed. She stood silent as he took her hands in his and continued with his declaration, his unrestrained passion in presenting it rendering her wordless.

"It has been said the gift of a rosebud is considered a confession of love. I should like to give to you all the rosebuds of this garden—nay, those of all the gardens in France! Tell me your heart does share mine's affections, that your soul shares mine's desires. I treasure you, my dear Rhianna, and I want to treasure you always. Grant me the permission to do so and cease this torment!"

No sooner had he avowed this last to her than a servant came racing toward them from the house. Once within audible distance, the servant exclaimed his winded announcement.

"Count Vallière, Miss Braden! I beg your pardon, but there is a guest arrived only a few moments ago. He comes from England for you, Miss Braden, and requests to speak with you on a matter of great importance! Marquis Vallière is with him and begs you to come directly."

The awkward interruption drained all color from Philippe's complexion, while Rhianna's cheeks flushed pink with embarrassment. After a weak recovery, Philippe recognized the need to put aside his proposal.

"Where are they?" he called out to the servant.

Rhianna was grateful for his response, for she was not yet lucid enough to form words of any audible quality. First, Philippe's declarations and, now, a mysterious visitor from England! She decided it imperative that she focus only on taking in each breath.

"The drawing room," the servant responded, with his first look of curiosity at the scene before him.

Philippe lowered his eyes to the hands he yet held and seemed unwilling to release them.

"You must go," he stated with chagrin.

Feeling severely for him and how his proposal had been so critically disrupted, she hardly knew how to respond, either to him or to the servant.

"Philippe…" His name was all she could manage and, yet, it said everything to him.

"Come," said he, with grand composure, "we shall *both* go."

There could be no other option. They withdrew from the garden and hastened toward the house.

•••

His arrival was early in the day and unannounced, but Guilford, Lord Kingsley, received a warm reception to the Vallière home. A strikingly tall man, with a broad stature and a generally pleasing appearance, he entered the Vallières' drawing room with little time for social graces. With a brief introduction and hurried civilities, he explained his visit from England to Marquis and Marquise Vallière.

"I hope you will forgive the discourtesy," he expressed. "It is unfortunate that we must meet in this manner, but the tidings I bring are rather urgent."

Even under such circumstances, Lord Kingsley had a composed way about him. His calm, gentle manner recommended him to Marquis Vallière who, although characteristically cautious and fittingly concerned, felt quickly at ease with this unknown traveler.

"Please, will you not have a seat?" insisted the somewhat rounder, though in no way displeasingly shaped Marquis Vallière. Turning to his butler, he instructed, "Belmont, do bring our guest some refreshments."

"I thank you for your kind hospitality, Marquis Vallière," Lord Kingsley replied somberly. "However, I feel I cannot rest until I have carried out the purpose of my visit. I bring a message to Miss Rhianna Braden. It is my understanding that it is here, in your excellent care, that I may find her."

Marquis Vallière was excessively protective of his children and, as he had for the last decade considered Rhianna as one of them, his first reaction to this comment was guarded.

"Of course," he responded, with a thoughtful nod. "I imagine this message is from someone of close connection to her."

"It is. I have personally been well acquainted with Miss Braden's father for many years and, in fact, bestowed him with the benefice at Thornton Church where Miss Braden lived prior to her schooling at Madame Chandelle's School for Girls."

"Ah! I see," he declared, his investigation nearly complete and his inquiring mind all but satisfied. "And I trust her father is well?"

Lord Kingsley hesitated before answering, "It is of Mr. and Mrs. Braden that my message refers. I am afraid it is not good news and, if it is not an unreasonable request, it is my hope that it be related first to Miss Braden."

"Oh dear," Marquise Vallière declared, speaking for the first time since their introduction. She wrung her hands together.

Marquise Vallière was a petite, slender woman whose exquisite fashion and irreproachable character were eclipsed only by her common sense.

"I do not believe Rhianna and Soleil have returned yet from their riding," she told her husband.

As she spoke her words, Soleil entered the room. Belmont closed the double doors behind her.

"What is it, Mother? You look troubled."

Soleil, noting the intensity in the air, turned to the unacknowledged guest. Marquis Vallière hurriedly introduced him.

"My dear, this is Lord Kingsley of Thornton, England. He is the friend and patron of Rhianna's father and wishes to speak with her *tout de suite*."

Stationed beside her mother, and at once afflicted, she offered, "Rhianna had mentioned going for a walk in the garden. To my knowledge, she is yet there."

A servant was dispatched to find her at once.

•••

Neither Rhianna nor Philippe wasted a moment. As the doors were opened and the two entered the drawing room, Rhianna moved instinctively toward Marquis Vallière, a man she had for many years viewed with a deep, fatherly regard.

"What has happened?" she implored him.

"There you are, child," he received her. "Rhianna, we have a Lord Kingsley to see you."

At the mention of this name, Rhianna's heart fluttered so intensely that she was certain it could not endure another surprise in the same day. Could she have heard him correctly? Lord Kingsley, owner of her most beloved Thornton, England manor house?

"I beg your pardon?" she replied.

The tall man beside her bowed—the most graceful bow she had ever witnessed—and she pressed her hand to her chest as if to ease the palpitations. When his posture straightened, she curtseyed with equal elegance and he took a step toward her.

"It is a pleasure to make your acquaintance, Miss Braden," he began, his voice kind and mild. "My only wish is that it would have been under happier circumstances."

Rhianna wondered only briefly if her outward appearance revealed the fusion of emotions within. This was the man, the *face* of the man, who inhabited so many of her dreams that even ten years in France could not allay, the man who invited her to balls and greeted her at the gates on many a wakeful night, *the man who lived in Kingsley Manor.*

"I come to inform you of an occurrence which brings me great pain to relay. Forgive me, for I know I shall never find the appropriate manner with which to report it."

Marquis Vallière stepped forward. "Perhaps we should excuse ourselves."

He motioned to his wife and children to leave so that Lord Kingsley might carry out his obligation with confidentiality, but Rhianna awoke from her reflections in time to intercede.

"No, pray, do not leave. Whatever Lord Kingsley has to say, he may say it before us all. Indeed, I prefer you stay," she said, turning to Lord Kingsley, "if it is not objectionable to you, my lord."

Guilford Kingsley showed no disapproval. "If that is your wish, it is entirely at your discretion."

"Thank you. Please, proceed."

He nodded in accord, and said, "Though we have never had the privilege of meeting, Miss Braden, I have been a friend of your father for a great many years. Therefore, I have taken it upon myself to personally bring you a message which, in my opinion, cannot be given by way of written word."

For the second time this day, Rhianna received a shocking announcement: a carriage accident, which Mr. and Mrs. Braden had not survived.

"When did it happen?" Marquis Vallière delicately questioned, as Philippe and Soleil assisted Rhianna to the nearest seat.

"Three weeks past," Lord Kingsley declared. "I left almost as soon as it was made known to me. Miss Braden, allow me to be among the first to offer my deepest of sympathies."

"Thank you," she responded, her voice barely above a whisper.

"Belmont, please, some water," Marquise Vallière requested, as she and her two children surrounded Rhianna.

Condolences were offered by the others, but she hardly heard them. Water was soon given her, but she was hardly aware as she sipped from her glass. Philippe's hands held one of her own, but little did she feel it. Her mind accepted the knowledge imparted by Lord Kingsley that funeral services had been carried out, but beyond this her mind could not process.

Emotionally fatigued, Rhianna soon retired to her room, not to emerge for the rest of the day and night. There seclusion afforded her a chance to reflect, however deliriously, on the day's events.

• • •

The horses moved gracefully through tall, wrought-iron gates, blithely pulling their two-wheeled *barouche* toward the manor. Bathed in the light of a beaming, springtime sun, they danced past the hedgerows that grew along the property's enclosing stone wall and up the familiar cobblestone approach.

Breathlessly, their passenger gazed from her window, clinging to her reticule. The landscape was vast and impressive, populated with meticulously placed shrubbery, spring flowers in full bloom and, in the center of the lawn, an ornate, Grecian fountain spurting forth its sparkling waters. It was just enough to distract her until the *barouche* pulled up to the front of the great Kingsley Manor.

At long last, the horses pulled to a stop. The driver stepped down and opened the carriage door, offering his hand to assist her. Accepting it with one slender, lace-gloved hand, she, too, stepped down, lifting her parasol high above her red curls and porcelain skin. After smoothing out her muslin gown, she raised her eyes toward the portico before her. She blushed, as the enchanting lord of the manor himself appeared to greet her.

Removing his top hat, he approached with a bow, and said…

"I regret to inform you Mr. and Mrs. Braden did not survive."

Rhianna jerked upright to a sitting position, her heart racing and her palms sweaty. A glance to the far wall revealed the tracing of a moonlit *escritoire* that reminded her of where she was. The familiar dream had taken a turn for the worse.

Gradually she took control of her erratic breathing, as the bedroom that had become home the last few years seemed to wrap its arms around her. Some hours yet remained before the sun would rise, but though she was inclined to fall back into her bedcovers and pull the white linens up under her chin, she feared what surrendering to sleep would bring.

She decided to seek comfort from the one object that, as a child, brought her peace in a foreign land—the only piece of England she still had. With the house and those in it sleeping soundly around her, Rhianna swung her feet over the side of the bed, lit a taper, and carried it to her dressing table.

Taking a seat on the ivory, embroidered cushion mounted on a mahogany frame, she placed the taper before the mirror and opened one of the small drawers. Lifting the brooch in her fingers, she examined the gold trinket from all angles as she had many times before.

Of course, it was more than a familiar ornament. Rhianna was wholly intimate with it, knew every stone, every change of hue in each of the pearls, its oval center a window to the past. Indeed, as she examined the object—a going away present from her dear, mysterious English friend—she could still hear the sound of the impending carriage coming to take her away from the only world she had ever known.

Memories of the past held her captive for a time, but she at last returned the brooch to the drawer. Her home was here now, and despite the sadness that had loomed over Rhianna's young life, her broken heart had healed by rooting itself, not in England, but in France.

Suddenly, raising her eyes to her reflection in the mirror, she was at once startled to see the likeness of her nine-year-old self looking back at her. Rhianna leapt to her feet as the same fair skin, red curls, and green eyes met her, but with the appearance and innocence of her younger years.

And with a blink, that young girl's image was gone.

• • •

Lord Kingsley's intention to reserve a room at a nearby inn was at once overthrown by the Vallières. It was quickly settled that the two weeks he intended to remain in France would be spent with them at the *manoir*.

During the course of the next several days, Rhianna recovered enough to speak with Lord Kingsley at length about the accident. She was glad when, finally, she could express her appreciation for his coming to France. To her consternation, however, as the shock of her parents' death wore off, Rhianna discovered an unsettling truth: that other than said initial shock, she felt very little. This troubling find left her questioning her very humanness, and even many hours of meditation could not open her to forgive the coldness of her heart.

Despite a dark cloud of self-condemnation looming over her, Rhianna found speaking with Lord Kingsley a welcome respite. Always interested in the lives of those who resided in Kingsley Manor, she was eager to hear him speak of its mistress, Lydia— Lady Kingsley—and of their two children, Desmond and Audra. As the days continued to pass, Lord Kingsley transformed from the fictitious creature of her imagination to a real person—and a good-natured, sympathetic one at that. Rhianna soon hoped to learn from him, indeed, to emulate the apparent goodness in this man, who showed gracious attentiveness even to her own inconsequential account of life in France.

At dinner one evening, shortly after his arrival, Lord Kingsley made Rhianna an offer she could hardly refuse. Indeed, he told her it was an offer he always intended to make, but had hesitated for fear of overburdening her: If she wished, he would be glad to personally escort her back to Thornton, England. More than that, Guilford Kingsley completed his invitation by including a place to stay at his own Kingsley Manor.

"Kingsley Manor! Do I understand you correctly?" she asked across the table.

"For as long as you wish," he told her, as a servant offered Philippe a clean fork to replace the one he had dropped to the floor.

Rhianna had not been to Thornton since she was a nine-year-old girl. Moreover, she was not devoid of a desire to return once again, though she quickly reproached herself for having such narrow-minded reasons as seeing her place of birth and staying at Kingsley Manor. After all, there was the matter of cleaning out her parents' cottage to consider, though she was certain there would be nothing of sentimental value within. And, of course, as Lord Kingsley suggested, she may wish to pay her respects to the deceased.

"That is very generous," Marquis Vallière said, followed by his wife's echoing sentiments.

Soleil, the only one at the table who knew just how large an offer this was to Rhianna, mirrored her mother's feelings and caught her friend's hand under the table with an excited squeeze.

"Lord Kingsley, I hardly know what to say," Rhianna replied, setting her wineglass down on the table without taking a sip.

"You should seriously consider it," Marquis Vallière encouraged. "After all, we are not going anywhere."

"No, we are not," Philippe said.

Rhianna understood *his* meaning at once, and was, in fact, the only one to understand him. Neither she nor Philippe had discussed his interrupted proposal from that fateful morning with anyone, nor had he broached the subject again with her.

Collecting herself, Rhianna tried not to be dazzled by the idea of living at Kingsley Manor and considered her life in France. Here was her home, and besides the lure of the manor, what did Thornton hold for her?

"Lord Kingsley, I do hope you will give me some time to think it over," she said.

"Take all the time you need," he answered. "The option is there, if you wish to accept."

As the night wore on, Rhianna became increasingly aware that a fascination with returning to England was strong within her— not to mention the prospect of fulfilling her childhood dream of not only stepping foot in Kingsley Manor, but *living there*. Nevertheless, the notion of leaving France, where she had made both a home and a family, was a melancholy one. Moreover, there was Philippe's confession of love to consider...

But the prospect of marrying Philippe frightened her terribly— and is that what one ought to feel after receiving a proposal from an agreeable gentleman? Rhianna suspected not, and her suspicions grew stronger as Soleil's fascination with Armand grew daily. Of course, if she rejected Philippe, Rhianna could not help but wonder what she would do if Soleil were to marry. Under such circumstances, would she find reason to remain in France? Or, was marrying Philippe the only sensible option for a woman in her position? The Marquis and Marquise seemed to be very happy together; perhaps she could have something similar with Philippe.

On the other hand, what could England possibly hold for her? And would she ever forgive herself if she did not go?

• • •

Marquise Vallière and Soleil had immediately seen to it that their dressmaker prepare the necessary mourning wardrobe for Rhianna, and on the day following Lord Kingsley's offer to accompany Rhianna to England, the first of three outfits was completed. Thus smothered in layers of black *crêpe*, Rhianna decided to debut her dreary new costume with a turn through the garden.

She was not there long when Lord Kingsley appeared. "Miss Braden, may I have a word?"

Always pleased to see him, the somber mood her clothing inspired quickly lifted at his arrival. "Good day, Lord Kingsley. Of course."

Guilford held his hands behind his back as he walked with her. The day was fine, as it had been the day Philippe professed his love. Rhianna was at once grateful that it was Lord Kingsley, and not Philippe, who accompanied her on her stroll.

"I believe you are aware that I bestowed Mr. Braden with the benefice at Thornton Church," he said to her.

To this common knowledge, Rhianna replied in the affirmative. "I am."

He paused before his next statement, but his countenance gave off a serious air. Rhianna got the distinct impression there was something more. As, in fact, there was.

"What you are no doubt unaware of," he said at last, clearing his throat, "is that I deeded it to him many years ago."

Rhianna stopped and turned to him. As she did so, her arms fell to her sides and her hands closed over folds of ebony fabric.

"I beg your pardon?"

179

Lord Kingsley supported his statement with a nod. "You are the sole heir, Miss Braden. The benefice is now under your control."

Rhianna realized suddenly that she was staring. Quickly returning her eyes to the path, she began to place one foot carefully in front of the other. He followed her.

"I hardly know what to say, Lord Kingsley."

"Then you have already fulfilled my request." As she turned to him yet again, he continued, "It is not public knowledge that such is the case. In fact, at the time the matter transpired, it was under the stipulation that it remain, for all intents and purposes, a private transaction. I had my own reasons for doing so, and I'm sure you will understand I cannot elaborate."

Rhianna mumbled something in agreement, though she hardly knew what.

"Miss Braden," Lord Kingsley went on, "obviously, no one could foresee the sad situation that has now befallen us. I must admit to you, though, I did not anticipate the matter of the benefice coming to light at this time."

He paused, and Rhianna felt the necessity of a response.

"I'm not entirely sure I comprehend you," she admitted.

"It is my wish," he told her, discreetly scanning the garden around them, "for the time being, that the general understanding continue to be that the benefice is Kingsley property. I am hoping that in placing this delicate situation in your confidence you might be willing to work with me." Lord Kingsley drew a long breath, and added, "I realize you would have no reason to grant this peculiar request of mine. Furthermore, you have not been of my acquaintance for more than a week…"

"Lord Kingsley," Rhianna said, incited by her clearer understanding, "please, say no more. We may not have known each other for very long, but I am forever indebted to you for overseeing my parents' funeral arrangements. Not only that, but your kindness in traveling to deliver the tragic news of their passing to me personally will not be forgotten. Whatever your reasons, it would seem to me the least I could do. In fact, I would be happy to oblige."

Rhianna saw him suddenly release the tension that had been in his shoulders and his arms relaxed at his sides. He smiled at her.

"Thank you, Miss Braden. It is…of great relief to me."

They walked on in silence as Rhianna considered the impact this would have on her decision of whether or not to leave France.

"I imagine, then," Rhianna said, as if thinking aloud, "I have no choice but to go to England."

"Well, that all depends," Lord Kingsley said, "on how involved you wish to be in selecting a new clergyman. The extent of your participation, of course, is entirely up to you."

"Lord Kingsley," Rhianna confessed. "I do not pretend to know the first thing about choosing an appropriate clergyman."

"I will be happy to make my recommendations to you, either in person or by post."

Rhianna's head swirled. This added an entirely new element to her situation, and not one that in any way simplified matters.

"Well, Lord Kingsley, it would seem I have quite a lot to think about and I suspect a bit of tea is in order."

"May I accompany you back to the house?"

Feeling a bit overcome by her thoughts, Rhianna was glad to take his arm and make her way with him back to the *manoir*. That she would have control over the benefice was of itself enough to fuel her recent insomnia, but Lord Kingsley's request for silence even more so. After all, what reasons could a man have to deed away property and then fear its discovery?

It would be difficult, but she resolved to curtail her mind's wandering until she was out of his presence.

• • •

Near the end of Lord Kingsley's two-week visit, the choice of whether to remain in France or return to England was still not made. The evening before Rhianna had to decide, she and Soleil politely stayed with the party after dinner for only as long as was socially necessary before excusing themselves to escape upstairs.

Soleil privately hoped she might persuade Rhianna to go to bed early. The latter had been up nearly every night since Lord Kingsley came and Soleil began to fear for her friend's health. But, as with all previous nights, she was unsuccessful. When it had grown late, Rhianna protested against Soleil's continued companionship, declaring it was unnecessary for both of them to lose sleep.

"As if I could go to my room and get a moment's sleep," Soleil professed. "I could hardly think of leaving your side while you are in this weakened state."

"I will be fine, Soleil, you really mustn't stay."

"You know the depth of my affection for you, Rhianna. I am going to stay in this room tonight and do not expect me to change my mind."

Soleil knew Rhianna had no energy to persist in urging her, and clearly it would be a fruitless venture. She smiled as Rhianna accepted with a sigh.

"I do not know how I am supposed to feel, Soleil," Rhianna declared, at length. "You know better than most that I never was close to my mother and father. If I return to England and visit their graves, it will be out of a sense of obligation only, to do what is right and honorable."

"Of course, we support any such endeavor."

"But I have no *attachment* to them, Soleil. That is the difficult thing. Of course, news such as this is shocking, and I still hardly believe it, but they did not love me, as you and your family have."

"You must not say such things," Soleil told her delicately. "I have no doubt they cared for you very much."

"If such was the case," Rhianna declared, with only a trace of the inner regret and heartache she had long suppressed, "they neither demonstrated it nor declared it."

To this, there was nothing to be said, for her words had been proven true in the many years of little correspondence. The few letters sent, always in her father's hand, bore no measure of feeling and, in ten years, not one visit was requested of her, nor performed on their part.

Soleil fell to the seat of the rosewood vanity, her body facing away from the mirror, her arms draped across the back of the chair. Without any convincingly positive response, she remained silent and watched with uneasiness as Rhianna sat curled before the great bay window of the room, gazing blankly into the moonlit countryside.

The hours passed and fatigue set in. With so much to meditate on, conversation continued intermittently. Soleil was glad amidst the tragedy to observe Rhianna's emotions had not crumbled beneath her. Rather, her demeanor was merely solemn, reflective.

But Soleil was yet unaware of a matter of particular significance.

The words that caused Soleil suspicion did not come until nearly twelve o'clock. They came subtly and were peculiar enough in character that one would naturally be inclined to reflect on them for meaning. Rhianna, drowsy and incoherent, spoke them aloud unwittingly, saying, "He would not wait for me."

All at once, Soleil had a sense that there was something more—an underlying element troubling her friend. She could not seem to place Rhianna's words in accordance with any subject that had distressed them as of late. After some time pondering this sentiment, she came to no sensible explanation.

"You must forgive my presumptuousness, Rhianna, but I must know," said Soleil, "is there something you have not told me?

Indeed, I know you too well not to discern you have something else vexing your thoughts."

Rhianna turned to her somnolently. Soleil moved toward her and seated herself beside her friend on the sill. She said nothing, so as to allow her sisterly companion a moment to collect her thoughts.

"My dear Soleil," she began, "I should never have imagined you *not* to discern as much, and I confess I am grateful for it. I so wanted to tell you, yet I could not seem to find the words on my own. Even now, I can hardly begin."

Soleil, though anxious, refrained from interrupting and gave her a moment to continue with her delirious reflection.

"But I suppose it no longer matters," Rhianna sighed, "for I am to be in mourning for a whole *year*."

Soleil held her breath, wondering at the implications, while Rhianna faded in and out of aberration.

"What no longer matters, Rhianna?" she implored.

"Why would Philippe ever want to wait an entire twelvemonth?"

The mention of her brother's name all but confirmed her suspicions.

"Do you mean to tell me," Soleil cried, with a start, "that *Philippe has proposed?*"

Her last words were uttered an octave higher than those at the start of her question and Soleil covered her own mouth at the realization of it. Simultaneously, Rhianna's full mental powers appeared to return and both women listened intently to the silence around them. Fortunately, the house remained silent.

"Yes," Rhianna replied at first. "No," she retracted suddenly. "That is, he *attempted* to before he was interrupted."

"Gracious God, when?"

"The morning after the dance, after you and I parted at the stables, Philippe met with me in the garden. It happened moments before Lord Kingsley's arrival."

Soleil was quite struck by this and considered Rhianna with great admiration for speaking of it with such fortitude.

"What awful timing, Philippe! Oh, Rhianna!"

"You were right all along! How could I not have known? It was all so obvious, you must wonder at my naïveté." Rhianna continued, "I can only imagine that he will now withdraw his offer."

"Oh, for shame, Rhianna! There is nothing to reconsider as far as *you* are concerned. I congratulate him on choosing so amiable a girl! As to withdrawing his offer, you misjudge him severely. I know my brother very well. He would not wish to detach himself because of your changed situation. Philippe is far too loyal. He will wait."

Another silent pause ensued, this one being longer than the last. Finally, Soleil asked the question which was to complete her understanding of the situation.

"Rhianna, forgive me," she began delicately, "but there is one more thing yet to ask, and do tell me, please, if I am being too curious." Rhianna gave her full attention, and Soleil inquired, "As to *your* feelings…regarding Philippe?"

She stopped, but that Rhianna understood her meaning was clear as her cheeks flushed with color.

"I do care for him, Soleil," she confessed, at length, "though I always felt my affection was of the most sisterly kind. But he is so good-hearted and generous to all, and he cares so strongly for the welfare of those dear to him. It is so contrary a demeanor to that of any I have come across in all my male acquaintances." She paused, before adding, "I think I do not deserve him."

"*That* is not true. But, do not imagine me to be excessively partial toward him," Soleil expressed with all honesty. "*We* shall be sisters with or without him, so if you do not share his feelings, do not hesitate to say so. I shall not be offended."

With a moment's further reflection, Rhianna said, "Although I have confessed nothing to him, Soleil, I believe I could very well love Philippe."

• • •

The following morning, despite much tossing and turning, and little sleep, Rhianna arose early, her decision made at last. Below, she could hear a stir in the morning room. The others, too, it seemed, had arisen early and were already downstairs. Dressing quietly, so as not to wake Soleil, she hurried to greet them.

As she entered the room, she was surprised to find that everyone was *not* already gathered there. Instead, she found only Philippe was up and about.

"Oh! Philippe," she declared, startled to find him standing by the window. He turned immediately toward the sound of her voice, as she said, "I have intruded on your solitude, forgive me."

She turned to withdraw from the room, but he stopped her.

"Not at all," he quickly returned. "Pray, do not leave. My solitude has, in fact, been dragging for some time now and I would be glad of your company."

Rhianna was certain it to be the most uncomfortable moment she had ever known. Ordinarily, she was never timid before Philippe. Indeed, she had always felt a sense of ease in his presence. But this morning was different. After all that had passed, she knew not how to conduct herself.

"Please, I beg you," he further entreated, taking some few steps in hesitant advancement toward her. "Stay."

At last, she moved to the window and stood beside him, as she would normally have done in this same circumstance, but resolved to keep her face inclined toward the window, her only retreat from the uneasy situation.

After a long moment overlooking the estate grounds where she and Soleil had last ridden two weeks prior, she commented, "While I am away, I shall remember the *manoir* just as it is today, the house and everything surrounding it bright and sunny."

With this confirmation of her decision to go to England, she felt Philippe's eyes upon her.

"Strange," he replied somberly, "how the most bright, sunny day could be so hideously drear."

A great sadness fell over her and her gaze blurred. As she allowed her fingers to play languidly with the curtain, a single tear slid down her cheek. Anxious to hide her emotion, she raised her hand to remove it, but Philippe interceded. Enclosing her fair hand in his, he eased her toward him and kissed the small tear away.

"I never expected that such a day would come when you would leave us," he told her, regaining control over his own emotions and shifting to his proper distance from her. "Nor did I imagine how intolerable it would be for me if you went away."

"Philippe, please, you must not say such things," she struggled. "It will make it more difficult for me to go." As she spoke, she could not raise her eyes to his.

"And what of me? Am I doomed to return to that cursed silence which has anguished me all these years?" He pleaded, "Let me speak, and find forgiveness in your soul, indeed, pity me, for if I do *not* speak, I will die within, broken of spirit and broken of heart. Rhianna, can you not feel how this house is already in despair with the pains of its loss?"

His words pained her deeply, as another tear fell, and then, another.

Philippe concluded his plea, saying, "My selfishness is overtaking me on this matter, but I know not how to hide my distress at your leaving. We need you here, Rhianna. Soleil needs you here. *I* need you here."

His straightforward manner, his unswerving resolve to discuss the only subject she was ill prepared to reflect on, caused Rhianna the greatest of consternation.

With effort, she declared, "You speak as though I am never to return."

Its effect was hardly that for which she hoped, as he replied, "And I venture to say you will not. As I stand here before you, I can see the future. You will go, and you will meet an Englishman, and you will fall in love…"

"Philippe!"

"Since we were children together," he continued, with vehemence, "I have had it in my heart that you would be my wife. Will you deny me of all hope? Deny me my only meaningful wish?"

Rhianna took a moment to collect her thoughts and emotions. "Surely, I need not remind you of my situation, Philippe. My connections are poor…"

"Your connections mean nothing," he cried, his own emotions overtaking him. "It would not change my feelings if you sold flowers on the streets of Paris. *Nothing* could ever change my feelings."

The two stood for a few moments in agonizing silence. Wishing only to escape from the morning room, Rhianna prayed there might appear an opportunity for release.

"Philippe," she told him, at last, "I dread to think of how I will get on without you all. But I feel it is my duty to pay my respects to my parents. Surely, you understand."

Philippe nodded. "Rhianna," he gently responded, a choking sound in his throat, "if that were all, then you not being a part of our lives for a time would be far more bearable. But I fear we are in danger of losing you for good."

This concept brought animation to Rhianna's person and she found courage enough to raise her eyes to meet his.

"What a notion! What reason could I possibly have to remain in Thornton once my obligation is finished? I have nothing holding me there, Philippe."

"What is it that holds you here, Rhianna?" he asked, his hand still wrapped around hers.

With this, she knew Philippe was hoping for some small confession on her part, but something held her back. She *did* love Philippe, she always had, but love has many forms. And, deep within her heart, did she not feel he deserved better than a curate's daughter? Though he would not admit it, as far as Philippe was concerned, it would be a poor match. Rhianna suspected that some time away from Manoir Vallière to think might be beneficial for them both. In the meantime, she resolved not to allow him the opportunity for his affections to be alleged further.

"*Everything* holds me here. France is my home," she declared. "It grieves me very much to go; it shall be sorely missed."

Philippe raised the back of her hand to his lips before releasing it.

"And you, my dear Rhianna, will be painfully missed in return." He concluded, "You must come back to France. I will not hear of it otherwise."

Voices were soon heard descending from the upstairs chambers. To Rhianna's great relief, it was only moments before Marquis Vallière, his wife, Soleil, and Lord Kingsley were all assembled together with them, ending what was to be her last private conversation with Philippe before her departure.

• • •

It was soon settled. Rhianna Braden would return to Thornton, England and reside as a guest at Kingsley Manor. With her bags quickly packed, everyone gathered together in front of the Vallière home to see her off the very next morning.

Still overwhelmed with the developments of the last fortnight, Rhianna, dressed in black bombazine, bid dreamlike farewells to her surrogate family. The picture seemed an illusion as she took trancelike steps toward a halted *barouche*, the door opened for her entry.

As the coachman pulled away, Soleil and Philippe were the last to return to the house. In fact, Rhianna did not see them return, for a hill obstructed her vision. But Philippe stood outside that sad home long after Rhianna's carriage disappeared from sight.

About the Author

Amanda L. V. Shalaby's passion for all things Jane Austen was inspired by her mother and grandmother. She now writes her own English historical romances and her debut novel, *Rhianna*, was published in July, 2012. When Amanda is not writing, she enjoys spending time with her husband, Matthew; her Shih Tzu dogs, Isabella Jane and Huntley Rochester; and her Persian cat, Sebastian.

9 781440 567094